LATER BLOOMER

ALSO BY GRAYDON MILLER

Hostages of Veracruz
The Havana Brotherhood

LATER BLOOMER

GRAYDON MILLER

Tales from Darkest Hollywood

Grady Miller Books

Many stories appearing in this volume previously appeared in serialized form in **www.canyon-news.com**

Please contact the publisher at:
    gradymillerbooks @gmail.com

1236 1/8 N. Cahuenga Blvd.
Hollywood, CA 90038

First Edition

CONTENTS

Day of the Lotus

Sergeant Carmichael was badass. Before I went into Runyon Canyon undercover, she sent me to the Yale School of Yogic Arts in Van Nuys to bone up on kundalini. At least I could bluff my way through a yoga class: "Close your eyes and just say *om*."

That's how I met Fay Greener, alias Sri Faye. The winsome 19-year-old greeted me after class held on the lawn at Runyon. Turned out she had known Yogi Jeff, the latest in the recent in the string of yoga teacher deaths. Faye had a misty blue come-hither look and very nice asanas.

"Namaste."

"Jai guru dev."

"You don't say."

I immediately knew I had fallen for Faye. Hard. Before I knew what was happening I was saying yes to her invitation to a little hash house in Pasadena called the Crown of India.

I was afraid I'd blow my cover with the squad car, so I went through the motions of hotwiring it.

Crime turned her on. Faye and I had to pull over on the Pasadena Parkway and have wild reiki sex: you don't touch each other but it's very spiritually fulfilling. There was something fishy about the Crown of India from the get-go: the letter C- that the health department had plastered out front had been doctored with a marker, turning it into a C+. Inside the curry-scented dump, they were playing bad sitar covers of Karlheinz Stockhausen. I felt queasy even before trying the food.

The waiter took our orders, Faye first. From what had happened to Yogi Jeff at Runyon Canyon I knew to steer clear of the chicken korma. Victim #6 was stricken after eating some chicken korma— bad stuff, the kind of *E. coli* to make your nose fall off. I played it safe and ordered chicken khorma.

"Why did you do it, Faye?" I said. Her come hither look turned frosty. "You ordered paneer fried rice instead of the korma?"

"I was feeling vegan today."

She eyed me suspiciously.

"Let's try a little side order of satya. You dig?"

"Satya, truth." She put down her napkin and raised her eyes, now go-to-hell eyes. I had her right where I wanted her, and she started to sing.

"The Iyengar school is being edged out in Beverly Hills, Westwood and downtown by Ashtanga, power yoga. The world is out of balance. We need a place for peaceful, passive yoga based on pranayama, breathing."

"Well you didn't have to infect all the yogis with *E. coli*. Jeff, Rob, Pete, Tiffany, Bonnie and Clyde. Or flaunt your bilingual redundancy. I—*yo*—play that game, too, *dos*."

2

Her eyes grew mistier. "My next victim," she choked up, "was to be Yogi Bear."

"Great scot!!"

"No, Yogi Bear."

"Why did you have to do it, Faye? You could have flooded the Ashtanga studios with bad reviews. You could have alleged a lot of personal injury hooey, including torn ligaments, damaged vertebrae, slipped disks and lowered hubris. You could have still respected human life, Faye. Your victims were yoga-mat-toting charlatans, but they're people, too. I know that's hard to swallow."

Again she turned her come-hither peepers on to me. I melted like a Hershey bar in the Mojave.

"Faye, I bet you could tie a man into Freudian slip knots without even half trying."

"How do you know, Lama Tod?"

"Just a hunch. But there's one thing I need to know before surrendering to your wicked ways. Why all these victims?"

"Wilbur," she said. "My brother Wilbur came out here from Kansas City with big dreams. He wanted to set up a homeopathic pharmacy and wipe out polio."

"But polio has already been wiped out."

"Lama Tod, I don't get my kicks out of stomping on somebody's dream. . . Ashtanga was just too much for his weak-chinned, four-hundred pound carcass. All that stretching and standing on his head. Poor Wilbur."

"Lost him? Heart gave out?"

"No, the floor collapsed and he fell into a sweatshop below."

"And that was all she wrote."

"Wilbur got stitched into the racing stripes on jogging pants. And then got shipped to Sarasota, Florida, where he works in a Radio Shack. He now weighs 127 pounds. He went from kapha to vata body type quicker than you can say *yug*, Sanskrit for to join, to connect. I blame Ashtanga for killing the Wilbur I knew."

Faye. . . her come-hither gaze was now tarnished by tears. The poor thing was a sick puppy, alright. We booked Faye on eight counts of murder and attempted murder of me by food poisoning. She would be off the streets for at least a few weeks, and I would have enough time to figure out where the hell hither is.

The $10,000 Pooch

$10,000 REWARD for LOST DOG

Name: BOKU, Breed: SHIBA INU Sex: Male, Tail: Curls up and tip bends to the right. Size: Medium-Small (18 inches high, 28 lbs.), Color: Light tan with White Chest, Age: Born in 1996. Escaped from our Chinese friend's house in Monterey Park, California on Sept. 5, 2002 when we were out of town. Boku's home is in Silverlake. Boku could be carried by car to any city. Needs medication. We have distributed 20,000 flyers from door to door and to countless TV and radio stations. We are senior citizens but won't stop searching until we see him. Please keep this flyer until 2016.

—Flyer seen posted in Runyon Canyon

"$10,000 by Monday," said Mr. Big, coolly, "or you can expect a new visit from these gentlemen." Calling their likes 'gentlemen' was an oxymoron; they were a walking advertisement for Darwin's theories. "If you have any attachment, sentimental or otherwise, to your kneecaps, I would advise you to cough up the dough. Pronto."

With a curt nod from Mr. Big, the bodyguards hotfooted it down the wooden stairs of Doug and Valeria's shabby garage apartment. When they were gone, a pool of flop sweat remained below Doug's sneakers. (Upon closer inspection the sweat appeared to have a yellowish tinge.) A cogent, lucid person would have grabbed a mop, but Doug and Valeria, strung out on Snapple and unnerved by Mr. Big's visit, were anything but cogent.

Their knees went wobbly, and recriminations followed:

"It all started with that Pell Grant for phony Beautician's College," Doug reproached.

"There was no way for me to know it wasn't fully accredited. . ."

"Well, it wasn't what your mother had in mind when she said she wanted you to finish college," Doug snapped.

"Look at you, Mr. AFI. Your graduate screenwriting program really put us in a hole."

Doug put his hands to his temples in a bereaved expression so extreme as to bring Edvard Munch back from the grave to paint it.

"These are dangerous people," Valeria said. "You should have thought twice before you dropped out of the screenwriting program."

"Let's take Zoe out for a walk," Doug suggested.

"That's your answer to everything: an argument over credit cards, take Zoe for a walk, a nuclear reactor has leaked contaminants in the topsoil, take Zoe for a walk."

"Why don't we get married, Val? We argue just like married people."

Outside they went and trudged up the hill and through the rusty gates of Runyon Canyon, Zoe leading the way. As the trail became steeper under their feet, out the corner of his eye, Doug saw a paper on a bulletin board with a '1' followed by a lot of zeroes, and both eyes came elastically back to the flyer with the sure snap of a red ball returning on its rubber tether to the wooden paddle. Ten thousand clams for a lousy lost dog!

"If we had a shiba inu...," said Valeria wistfully, "we could get Mr. Big off our back."

"But we do have a shih tzu."

"Shiba inu and shih tzu are almost spelled the same."

"Yes, but she doesn't look anything like the shiba inu."

"A lot of time has gone by since 2002," said Doug. "A lot can happen in five years. So the dog got smaller, it changed into a different breed.

"Wait, wait," said Valeria.

She remembered a hairdresser who owed her some favors. She gave him a cheat sheet in beautician school. He'd aced the pedicure exam, thanks to her.

"Rodrigo owes me."

They went to the salon on Las Palmas, near Sunset, and asked Rodrigo for a favor.

"Can you do a big dye job?" Valeria asked after they hugged effusively, and she got pricked by his multiple body piercings. "It's top secret, very on the DL."

"How big?" he replied, sweeping up hair from the floor at day's end.

Just then Doug came into the shop with Zoe on a leash. The shih tzu barked *ruff ruff*. Rodrigo took one look at the canine and rolled his eyes. His eyes rolled right back into his skull and his head hit the base of a salon chair as he came down in a dead faint, hitting the floor with a thud.

As the eyes of the swooning hairdresser fluttered back open, Doug shoved the missing dog flyer in his face. Below "$10,000 REWARD" in bold letters appeared a fuzzy snapshot of a hound with white and tan patches, and demented red eyes.

"Rodrigo, it has to look just like that," Doug said. "Can you do it for us?"

"Sorry," he groaned, "I cut class the day they taught us how to make red contact lenses. Why are you doing this, if I may ask?"

"You know how they have casting agents for children?" Valeria said. "Our neighbor is a pet agent. He got my dog a part in a movie as Lassie's double."

"You can't fool me," Rodrigo said, wagging a finger. "I know what you're up to. Yeah. I see you two lovebirds, you want to collect the reward for the missing dog and get married. The money's been holding you back."

Doug glanced nervously, Valeria tittered, and Rodrigo started combing out Zoe's stringy fur.

Dyeing a four-legged animal was to an ordinary dye job what piloting a 747 is to traveling in one. Rodrigo sweated bullets as the skittish dog kept shaking the peroxide off its neck fur. It spattered onto Rodrigo's designer jeans, outré silk shirt and stung his skin. He squealed at each harsh drop. Finally, utterly defeated, Rodrigo sat on the floor and hyperventilated as Zoe ran circles around the salon.

"Let's nail her to the floor," Doug suggested.

Rodrigo, a devoted animal lover, protested fiercely.

"How would you like it if you had your feet nailed to the floor? It's cruel, inhuman, degrading. . ."

"OK, let's try super glue," Doug suggested. "I have some right here."

Doug was a guy who always carried around a backpack with everything you need: an Allen wrench, WD-40, a Swiss Army knife, a tube of super glue, and even a battalion of the Swiss Army. With great dexterity obtained as an Eagle Scout, Doug quickly managed to weld his own hand to the floor with super glue.

The mishap was a blessing in disguise. While the dog eagerly licked Doug's face, it stayed still long enough for the color to set.

By the time Rodrigo hosed off Zoe and shampooed the color out, she had white patches marbled with "honey-glow amber." The resemblance between her and the missing dog was astonishing.

"Well?" Rodrigo asked, cheerily manipulating a hand mirror around Zoe's hind quarters.

"Beautiful, Rodrigo," Valeria complemented him.

"I was talking to the dog," Rodrigo said.

"There is one teeny tiny problem, though," Valeria pointed out.

"Yes. . ."

"Zoe is a girl. The missing dog is a boy."

A collective sigh filled the salon.

"I think it's best we go home now," Valeria said to Doug, who still struggled to detach his hand from the floor.

"But we must believe," said Doug panting, "Ouch! This is pulling the skin off my hand. . . Yes, belief is the indispensable element."

"Get real," Valeria said. "We'd be just as likely to get a reward for a Pinks hot dog."

"You're scared, Val. That's what it is. You don't want to give up Zoe. You've had this dog since you were seven years old and Nana gave her to you. When she goes, she's gonna to leave a big empty place in your heart."

"Listen to Mr. Empathetic," Valeria snarled. "You can't wait to get rid of Zoe. Admit it. You always hated her leaving hairs on the couch, and slobbering in your *huevos rancheros*. But nothing will change the fact that Boku is a boy and Zoe is a girl."

Rodrigo could see tempers rising and shouted, "Time, guys."

Rodrigo, the peacemaking hairdresser with the Farah Fawcett bangs, placed his hands between the bickering couple and gently pushed them apart. Valeria glared at Doug, who in a burst of angry energy, had pried his hand, along with a linoleum tile, from the floor. Before anybody could say a word, Doug's mobile phone did the cha-cha-cha, and caller ID flashed the letters: M*r. B*i*g*.

"Valeria, get that," Doug barked. "It's awkward with a floor tile super-glued to my right hand."

She took the phone from its holster, and said, "Hello." Rodrigo watched, alarmed as Valeria's expression underwent a drastic change. She gulped, her face turned ghost-pale, and beads of sweat formed on her unlined forehead. Slowly handing the phone back to Doug, she said, "If we don't have the money by noon tomorrow. . ." That's as far as she got, before sobs truncated the thought.

"It's too awful," she wailed. "I can't tell you."

"Why can't you tell me?" Doug said. "There are no secrets between us."

Valeria took a deep breath and relented, "Mr. Big said they'd lock us in a room, alone, with Dia and Ray, the Hollywood Hills' hottest real estate team. He also promised a visit from a hooded stranger selling toupees."

"Nooooo!" Doug shrieked. "Mr. Big must have seen my therapist's files. He knows my phobia of signing disclosures and my recurring nightmare. As a child, I was deathly afraid of going to sleep. I had this frightening dream that the earth is attacked by giant toupees that terrorize the population and kidnap all the bald men on the planet. Yul Brynner would knock on our door, 'You've got to protect me kid. And whatever you do, don't let the toupees know I'm here.' One of the toupees came knocking at our door. They asked if there were any bald men in our house, I said no, cross my heart and hope to die if I should tell a lie. Then the toupees gave me some Tootsie Rolls, and I snitched.'

Valeria looked at Doug is if he were the guy in the bus, wearing a beanie with a propeller on top and spouting verses from "Howl."

"I thought there were no secrets between us," Valeria said. "I see I was sadly mistaken. It seems you like Tootsie Rolls."

"I didn't say that. I was a kid, and it was a dream. . ."

"The father of my children could never condone Tootsie Rolls. I'll tell you that right now, Doug," she said curtly. "We're wasting time. Rodrigo, get me the flyer for the dog."

She snatched it from Rodrigo's hand, and glared at the phone number and name of the dog's owners. Mr. Big's phone call had prompted an about-face in Valeria, who suddenly turned from this venture's number one doubter to its greatest booster.

"I think the dog's owner must be Armenian," she remarked, punching the numbers into Doug's phone. "Yes, hello, Mr. Fallopian," Valeria put on a cheerful but tentative voice. "We saw a flyer for your lost dog in Runyon Canyon. I think we may have him here. Me and my boyfriend found him. . . Are you all right, sir. . . Hello? Hello?"

"Please come to the house at once," Mr. Fallopian said between coughs and assurances that he was OK, and gave Valeria an address in Echo Park. After a few minutes of searching and questioning children on the street, they located the house, a modest bungalow. They rang the doorbell and waited. Again, they rang the doorbell. Finally, shuffling and coughing resounded through the nether regions of the house.

"Yes," said a wheezy, hostile voice from behind a closed door. Zoe, the painted shih tzu, made a low growling sound and bared her teeth. Nervousness oozed from their every pore; soon Doug and Valeria would be naked and vulnerable before the appraising eye of Boku's original owner.

"Whatever it is, I'm not buying," continued the voice behind the door. "And if you're these Jehovah people, you can pick up some mail from me that's going to my neighbor's house."

"Sir, we're here about your lost dog," Valeria said.

The door slowly opened, revealing the stooped man behind the wheezy, suspicious voice. "Dog? I have no dog. Years ago he ran away, a handsome shiba inu."

"We found him," Valeria said, her voice on edge.

"Are you sure you're not Jehovah's people?" Mr. Fallopian asked. "Do me a favor, will you? I've got some postcards for my neighbors. 'Aloha from Hawaii.' They'll eat their hearts out with envy when they see I went to the Waikiki Sheraton."

Mr. Fallopian looked toward the panting dog and his eyes narrowed.

"That's not my dog! That's some mangy two-bit, B-list Lassie stand-in."

Doug's and Valeria's hearts sank as the old man turned to go back into the house. "I'll be back with the postcards," he said.

"We're toast," Valeria said. "What can we do?"

Doug looked grim. Mr. Fallopian reemerged, and the dog, with contrasting patches of white fur and "honey-glow amber," ran forward, yapping and wagging its tail merrily. It ran forward and started licking Mr. Fallopian's hand.

Valeria noticed his eyes had the unregistering gaze of a blind man. "How I wish my Agnes were here to see this day," he was saying. "She passed a year ago in March. She was brave, I never heard her complain once about the cancer. Not once." Teardrops streamed out the crinkly corners of his unseeing, sun-faded eyes. "She was getting treatment, and it was under control. Then one day she was driving in our Caddie convertible on Robertson Boulevard. A cement-mixer driver mistook the Caddie for a condominium construction site. It was a shame. The thought keeps running though my head: if Agnes hadn't put off swimming lessons all those years, she might be with us today."

Seeing his distress, Valeria gave him a consoling hug. The blind man wept like a baby, and then started to French kiss her.

"Oh, I'm so sorry," Mr. Fallopian said. "I lost all decorum. It's been lonely without Agnes." He sniffled loudly. "But today is not the day to dwell on past losses. It is a day for rejoicing. Boku has returned."

Serenity and joy lit up the old man's face.

"What can I do for you? How can I possibly repay you for returning my dog?"

"Valeria nudged Doug. "Well, a $10,000 cashier's check wouldn't be a bad start," he said.

"A $20,000 cashier's check would be a better start," Mr. Fallopian said, smiling. "Alas, there is no more reward money. There were a lot of expenses to have Mrs. Fallopian's body jackhammered from the Cadillac."

As he spoke, Mr. Fallopian was petting the dog with great affection.

"You do feel a little shorter, Boku," he remarked. "And the tip of your tail doesn't bend as much to the right."

Valeria glanced at Doug apprehensively. They decided to leave the dog and the old blind man while their cloud of happiness remained intact. For Doug and Valeria, being able to give him the heart-kindling satisfaction of his dog's return was the greatest reward of all.

In a euphoric state they went back to their car. As they drove home, Doug inquired, "But don't you feel hurt that Zoe stayed so easily with the old man. After all, you had that dog since you were a child."

"If you love something set it free," Valeria said. "If it comes back, it will always be yours. If it doesn't come back, buy a new one."

"Val, I think I'd be peeved if I had an animal, washed it, and fed it year after year, and it ran off with a stranger."

"OK," she admitted, "I would have liked at least a whimper."

In the silence that followed, they felt something odd. Then a faint rustle made them jerk around and see a figure hulking in their back seat.

"Hello, my young delinquent student-loan holders," said Mr. Big, adjusting his bow tie. "Where's the ten grand?"

"We don't have it. . . on us," Doug stammered. "Let's go to the ATM."

"Don't pull that old trick," said Mr. Big. "You don't have it, and now you two can prepare to suffer torments, hideous, excruciating torments that Dante shrank from describing in his last circle of hell."

Doug and Valeria held each other's trembling hands, bracing for the worst.

"And now, by the authority vested in me by the Universal Life Church," said Mr. Big, "I now pronounce you man and wife."

(rare behind-the-scenes footage)

Rodrigo opened his eyes wide, disgruntled and indignant. "That wasn't really a motivated faint. The author was imposing his will. I feel ashamed. I'm thinking of withdrawing from this story altogether."

"I wouldn't do that," Valeria counseled. "We've got two more installments to go."

"We fictional characters have really got to unionize. It's up to us to raise the bar on dialogue and storyline."

"Let's get on with it," said Valeria. "I've got an audition at three o'clock with Joan Didion."

The Binge

The draft document, released by the American Psychiatric Assn., for the first time calls for binge-eating and gambling to be considered disorders, opening the way for insurance coverage of these problems. But it refrains from suggesting a formal diagnosis for obesity, Internet addiction or sex addiction, as some professionals had proposed.

Los Angeles Times, Feb. 10, 2010

Beanstock-thin Todd Harris attended, along with a gaggle of fashionably anorexic hipster moms, the meeting to plot a series of killer fundraisers to keep the hostile charter takeover of their boutique school at bay. The mere sight of Todd Harris, the apostle of mindful eating, the diet guru whose renown knew no borders, made the Jills and Jennifers fill their Chinette plates, albeit sparsely, with grapes and bananas and sunflower seeds; they chose Pellegrino water

17

over coffee, and cold-shouldered the fruit juices laced with high-fructose corn syrup. Nevermind the toothsome pastries brought by a gauche mom who was slightly out of the nutritional loop.

"West Hollywood Elementary's Fall Fundraising Blitz raked in beaucoup dollars," the chairwoman blathered away, as fidgety fingers sought the grapes and sunflower seeds. "Here at Hancock, it can work for us, too."

The smell of fresh-brewed coffee beckoned from a side table, and the tray of cinnamon rolls, set appealingly on paper doilies, looked so lonely, as the young mothers forsook them. A dozen cinnamon rolls topped by melting creamery butter, dripping into its crevasses, and spritzed by powdered sugar.

So lonely and forlorn they looked, the diet guru Todd Harris overcame his baggage of nutritional mores and grabbed a corner of the pastry coil. Nibbled on it. One nibble led to another nibble and another. . . Pretty soon the dozen cinnamon rolls diminished to nine. Todd wanted more; after his soul and stomach did brief battle, he devoured another cinnamon roll—"the last one," he reminded himself in the slightly unsure disciplinary tone reserved for his spoiled son. Meanwhile, one of the pudgier moms (.0001 percent body fat) was watching and commemorating on her cell phone camera as the diet guru broke all his rules.

1) Sugar and carbs will bring you to the cockroach level.

2) Eat with your mouth closed; it encourages mindful eating.

3) Eat sitting down at a table.

4) Stop at one of anything. (Having seconds are lethal to your girlish figure.)

Todd gobbled the cinnamon rolls with fiendish abandon, the creamy frosting smearing his lips, and he barely caught his breath between ravenous bites. After the meeting concluded, Todd Harris felt compelled to hit one of the doughnut shops on Santa Monica Boulevard. You could smell the rancid grease out in the parking lot. Showing one last shred of self-control, he asked for a bran muffin. Breaking law number 3, he ate sitting inside his German cabriolet—not at a table—and the crumbs cascaded onto the leather upholstery.

What a compromising position for a diet guru, one who had lost over one hundred and eighty pounds following his own program, and who was a walking advertisement for his revolutionary concepts! Still not having satisfied the yen for another cinnamon swirl and fearful of being seen in one of these dens of toxicity, he purchased a false mustache and a bottle of spirit gum. Looking rather like a young Burt Reynolds, Todd went into Magee's Donuts and ordered a half dozen cinnamon swirls smothered in whipped butter.

Thus commenced the binge. After three days, he had stopped going to his office. His belt was out a notch; a layer of jelly-like epidermal fat covered his once lean stomach, and self-loathing was a heartbeat away. When the doorbell rang, Todd was late to an important business meeting. On the intercom he confirmed the presence of one of the moms from Jake's school.

On the doormat stood Allegra Newton. Her hair frazzled, she looked like hadn't slept for a week.

"It's only a question of time before this goes viral," Allegra said abruptly after pleasantries were exchanged.

'This' refered to a portfolio, almost pornographically explicit, of Todd Harris' transgression. As Todd clicked on Allegra's cell phone, the snapshots shuffled past. Red flamed in Todd's pale cheeks, as if he'd been slapped when he saw himself: wolfing down the cinnamon rolls at the fundraising meeting: slinking into Yum Yum doughnuts: entering Magee's Doughnuts, disguised in a bushy mustache.

"What would it be worth to you to delete these embarrassing photos," the half crazed soccer mom asked Todd Harris. Dizzied from the slide-show of him gorging on cinnamon swirls and glaze-grottoed old-fashioneds, the diet guru was rendered speechless.

Todd Harris turned pale and ashen when he translated Allegra's words from crime novel cliché into plain English. The author of *Four Laws for a Better, Slimmer You!*, had had a marked aversion to Allegra Newton since attending a kids pizza lunch at his son's school. Allegra's pudgy daughter, Danae, was smitten by a second slice of pizza. When mom saw appear on Danae's plate a new slice laden with congealed cheese and pepperoni, she stared stonily. "But Mom," Danae whined. At once Allegra clawed the slice from the plate. The pudgy girl pleaded with her eyes. Like a man on death row the eve of his execution, Danae expected a last-minute reprieve for the pepperoni.

Allegra, with her adult notions of nutrition and demonized ingredients, dropped the pizza into the waste can. This is where an eating disorder starts, Todd mused.

He grew paler and whiter as the distasteful concept of blackmail seeped in.

"What are you asking?" he said under a shield of disingenuousness.

From the threshold of Harris' Hancock Park mansion, Allegra asked for a large sum of money outright.

"Sorry," he said, shaking his head sadly.

"Mr. Harris," she was unfailingly polite with her prey. "If these photos go public you'll be a naked hypocrite," Allegra said. "Telling people one thing, and doing another. Breaking every law of your Four Laws," she ticked them off on her satiny manicured fingers. "Carbs. Mouth open. Standing up. Having seconds, thirds, even fourths—"

"Don't you see, Allegra?"

"Don't Allegra me," she snapped.

"I was practicing law number 5—to be. . . "

"There are only *four* laws," she snarled.

"There's a fifth in the revised edition," he chipped in. "And. . ."

"Don't weasel out with your sophistries, Mr. Harris," Allegra cut him off.

"Sheesh, let me finish. . . The fifth law is to be OK with myself despite transgressions. Okayness is a key tenet of the Harris System."

"Nobody will buy that," Allegra said. "You're the guy who told Oprah, 'Coffee is God, sugar is the Devil.'"

Todd Harris nodded in remembrance: *Coffee is God, Sugar is the Devil* became the mantra for legions of overweight, stressed-out moms. His book rocketed to the top of the bestseller lists. Allegra was talking:

"I need fifty grand. Like yesterday."

"Read my lips. N-O," Todd said. "You can ask me a million times. The answer is still no."

Allegra put an interrogative, "million and one?"

"NOOOOO!" he exploded.

"Thirty thousand dollars," Allegra's lips quivered. "I can't go a cent lower."

Todd Harris's gaze sought the tile design on his doorstep.

"I'm in big trouble," Allegra whimpered, her hazel eyes tear-dazzled. "Big trouble. Because of my gambling. It started out in childhood. You know in Denny's, where you pay two quarters to guide the jaws of a toy crane over a bed of stuffed animals? From the stuffed-animal machine I graduated to Shakey's game room. It wasn't the pizza, I didn't even *like* the pizza; it was the Vegas allure of the tokens and games. From there it was a small step to Santa Anita. Last week Fallopian's Ghost was a sure thing in the fifth. The 10-1 choice finished a length behind, Hello Dalí. I took out a loan from a loan shark and bet it all, and now there's a hit on me. I'm being followed wherever I go. Mr. Harris, I'm beside myself. I'm. . ."

"You do need help," he said. "You know, the Diagnostic and Statistical Manual of Mental Disorders (DSM) from the American Psychiatric Association now contains binge eating and gambling as a mental disorder. Step inside," Todd said slowly, in an appeasing tone. "Let me get out my checkbook."

"Thank you, thank you, thank you," she bawled. "You're an angel, Mr. Harris. Please make the check out to the order of Bank of America."

Awed by the luxe, she took the first tentative steps into the sunken living room and took a seat. She looked around at the cathedral ceiling and Rodin sculptures. Waiting for the diet Guru to come back with the checkbook, she sat looking out a leaded glass window at a hummingbird stick its beak into scarlet blossoms—over and over, like a sewing machine needle going into cloth—she mused how the hummingbird must suffer an eating disorder. Then Allegra lurched violently forward, as she was nudged by the elbow of Rodin's Thinker squarely on the back of her head. Allegra sprawled on the floor, dead as a brick.

Todd Harris was taken aback as he reentered the living room, waving the Montblanc ink dry on the check. On the

Navajo rug in the living room lay the mother of one of his son's classmates, and she didn't appear to be breathing. *Murder in Hancock Park*—Todd Harris already pictured the bloated headlines—*Diet Doc Dusts Mommy*. Todd speed dialed Dr. Sheehan.

"Get over here, I need to see you. I think I killed somebody."

Who else? His chief head shrinker, his priest, his confessor and consigliore all wrapped up in one, Dr. Theodore Sheehan.

Dr. Sheehan, clad in tennis clothes and espadrilles, arrived shortly. Neglecting to shut the front door, Dr. Sheehan entered the foyer and stepped gingerly over the body at the head of the sunken living room. He beelined through the dining room and into the kitchen.

"What have I got to clean up for you this time, Todd?" he sighed.

"It was in self defense. Defending my career against this, this intruder. Listen," he cupped an ear.

"I hear nothing," Dr. Sheehan said.

"That's the sound of my empire crumbling."

Todd was dipping Pringles chips in French onion dip, one of his verboten foods, along with chimichangas and pork strudel. With a maniacal repetition, like a chain-smoker lights one cig after another, like a pothead joneses Doritos, he drowned tortilla chips by the fistful in creamy dip.

Slightly winded by the gorging, Todd made his way to the drawers and pulled out boxes of donettes coated by waxen chocolate and others sugar frosted. He opened the walk-in freezer and pulled out a side of beef. When he finished the chocolate donettes—his favorite—the white powder-sugar-frosted donettes had the effect of crop-dusting his cheeks and underlip in fine white powder.

"Donut?" he offered, his mouth full of sugary white mush.

"No thanks," replied Dr. Sheehan. "What are you doing stuffing your face? You're the holier than thou diet guru!"

"I'm doing research on the psychology of binging, for my next book," Todd said. "It's about to be considered a mental disorder."

"And that research included murder?" said Dr. Sheehan.

"It's a long story. . . Three parts."

"I'm listening," Dr. Sheehan said.

"Part one—embarrassing photos. Part three—murder."

Dr. Sheehan grimaced and clucked his tongue.

"Wait, Theodore, there's a golden parachute in here," Todd exclaimed. "She told me there was a hit out on her for her gambling debts. I'm sure we could get someone to testify, plant evidence. . ."

"Well," Dr, Sheehan replied, "as your psychiatrist and spin doctor, I suggest you immediately call a press conference. Show a willingness to face issues head on."

Within a snap of the fingers, the sedate Hancock Park manor was teeming with camera-wielding media troops. It flashed like a lightning storm in the Ozarks. A thirty microphone porcupine was shoved in Todd Harris's face as Allegra Newton's body showed in an unflattering light, her naked, cellulite-bound legs scissored unnaturally.

"Do you have a cocaine problem?" asked one journalist, with a French accent.

"No. I don't have a problem with cocaine. Got any?" When the press corps' chuckles faded, Todd continued: "That's not drugs," Todd gestured to the telltale white powder on his cheeks. "That's something much worse for a sanctimonious diet authority like myself. That's donut dust."

The press corps chuckled again. *If you want to get away with murder*, Dr. Sheehan had told him, *keep 'em laughing*. That advice was working. Todd now went on to explain how, his nerves were frayed by a blackmailer's demands, and he spiraled into a carb and pastry binge that culminated, unfortunately, in Allegra Newton's murder.

"I apologize to all those people I've hurt," he said. "I'm deeply, deeply sorry. I take full responsibility for my actions. It was very inconsiderate of me to pin Allegra Newton under Rodin's The Thinker."

Cameras clicked, the foyer buzzed with clambering hands and voices. Dr. Sheehan delivered a prepared statement:

"The Diagnostic and Statistical Manuel of Mental Disorders (DSM) from the American Psychiatric Association now contains binge eating as a mental disorder. Thus Mr. Harris intends to plead temporary insanity. And his defense team will make every effort to besmirch the good name of Allegra Newton."

Indeed, a jury composed of Todd Harris' peers—O.J. Simpson, Klaus von Bülow, Robert Blake and Richard Simmons—returned a verdict of not guilty by reason of insanity. He was the blameless victim of a murderous rage provoked by his eating binge, which was in turn provoked by stress, overwork and blackmail. The jury commended Todd for his rare forthrightness and honesty, and voted him a lifetime supply of Trader Joe's reduced guilt fudge brownies.

Call-Back

Speeding down Sunset Boulevard., in an embarrassing Toyota beater, Joel Bartlett noticed a voice mail waiting on his cell phone. Joel lost control of the wheel as he tried to keep one eye on the driving and another on his cell phone. The Toyota veered into the other lane, into the path of a Land Rover the size of Connecticut. Joel jerked out of harm's way in the nick of time and pulled to the side of the boulevard, and devoted full attention to retrieving the message.

It was Sidney, his agent, with an urgent call-back for a sitcom in Studio City. "They want you to read ASAP," Sidney said. The recurring character of the goofy neighbor with Tourette's Syndrome would endear him to a national audience and the steady stream of ka-ching would have a gaggle of financial managers working overtime, women in the grocery store would be ogling him, he would show the naysayers in Milwaukee he had been right to give up his job selling insurance and head west, and overnight his signature would turn into an autograph.

The elation turned to gloom when he realized the message was two hours old. While whiling away the afternoon in a dark, dank bar, nursing a lite beer and listening to Johnny Cash, Joel didn't hear the opening bars to "Hotel California," his ringtone. Why didn't he have the good sense to put the phone on vibrate? He'd learn from this blunder for next time, he reassured himself, but there was no next time. You blew it, you schmuck, he berated himself, you really blew it! It's back to Milwaukee for you.

Joel phoned Sidney to see if there was still a chance to report to the audition. "Joel, you schmuck!" his agent confirmed his own previous assessment of himself in an eardrum-piercing voice. "I'm dropping you as a client. I'm sorry. I'm no longer your agent." Just as Joel was to respond that he felt, in all fairness, he was more of a schlemiel than a schmuck, his phone died.

He lobbed the cheap phone out of the car window. Good riddance. He cursed the day that infernal device had come into his life. Then, seized by sudden remorse, Joel defied two lanes of lethal traffic to recover the phone, that contained his priceless Rolodex. Less than three feet away, a steel-belted tire belonging to a city bus flattened it to the width of pita bread.

Now, with the gas needle running dangerously low, he went to the sleazy electronic shop on Hollywood Boulevard where he had bought his phone. Joel slammed its steaming remains on the counter and bellowed, "This stinking phone made me miss a once-in-a-lifetime audition. I'd do anything to go back in time."

"Anything?" repeated the clerk with *Ali* stitched on his shirt and a dragon tattooed on the side of his face. Joel nodded yes. "Well then, I've got something that might interest you, boss."

Ali went into the back room, muttering to himself, and soon returned with a phone that was far from new. The strip of chrome was chipped off, its silver contours scratched like somebody had gouged it with a quarter.

"For one thousand dollars, my friend, it's yours."

"That piece of junk!"

"Listen, buddy, that's a bargain for the Chronos, Mark VII. Punch in the year, any year, and this baby will take you there. This will be the answer to all your troubles. From what I hear, this may be worth considerably more than a thousand clamshells for an actor with a sitcom in the balance. Believe me, I don't show this to all my customers."

"No kidding! What would they want with an old cell phone?"

"Listen to me. Press a date from the past, followed by the pound sign. And you will be tele-transported to that time and place, wherever you are standing."

"You're pulling my leg."

"Go ahead. Step onto the sidewalk and try it out." He added, "To return to the present, press the red button."

Joel hotfooted out of the store into the afternoon glare of Hollywood Boulevard, and punched in a date from a week ago. Something crackled and sizzled, and there was the faint smell of burnt hair and his scalp tingled. Joel crossed the street to a newsstand and scanned all the papers, they bore a date from a week ago. The Lakers still had a shot at the playoffs, and a righteous politician hadn't yet fallen from grace, and the weather forecast was dead wrong. Holy cow, the crazy thing worked!

Joel pressed the red "end call" button and, once delivered back to the present, purchased the tele-time-transporter faster than you could say déjà vu. "There is one condition of the Chronos Mark VII you should be aware of," said the salesman, Ali. "The time you use when you go back into the past, will be used up on this end in future."

"Sure, sure," Joel said, distractedly.

Ali asked, "Do you need a bag?"

Joel was already out the door. Excitedly he punched in the date of the fatal missed phone message. In a heartbeat he was surveying an assortment of gleaming Phaetons and Model A's, and hearing aooga horns on Hollywood Boulevard. He knew he got a wrong number, by a number of decades. In this bygone era his low-riding jeans, that revealed a strip of crimson-hearted boxer shorts peeking above the waist, caught the attention of an unlikely fashionista.

"Listen, buster," a beat cop snarled, twirling a whistle, "could you pull up those pants. Or would you like to get cited for showing a bit more of yourself than is decent?"

Joel obediently pulled up hits pants, mumbling, "My name's not Buster."

Across the boulevard, the sole feature to orient him was the corner newsstand. He threaded his way across the boulevard and dodged the crowded, clackety-clacking trolley cars. Reaching the newspapers, his eyes riveted on the date, March 13, 1938. Yikes, he'd robotically dialed his agent's number, 313-1938.

Despite his first instinct to press the red button and travel homeward to the comfort of the 21st century, he spied the alabaster face of a pretty young thing underneath the veil of a pill-box hat. His blood quickened and he instinctively followed her. He got ready to use one of his devastating pick-up lines when they both stopped, waiting for the crosswalk light to turn.

"Excuse me, I see you use shoes," he said, after finding a topic they shared in common. "I like using shoes. They're so good to protect your feet."

She turned to Joel, gazed deeply into his eyes, and said, "Nuts to you, Buster," and walked on. "My name's not buster," Joel said weakly. Stung by the rejection, he walked half a block and turned into a restaurant in the shape of a hat. The Brown Derby. Joel instantly recognized it from *I Love Lucy*. The maitre d' eyed him from the stellar height of some maitre d's Olympus. This guy was from central casting. His thyroid eyes rolled languorously, and he spoke in an intimidating German accent that made Joel feel slightly less dignified than vermin.

"Sir, that is not appropriate attire."

"Thank you for calling me 'sir'," Joel said. "I was beginning to think my name is Buster."

"Well, please put on a dinner jacket and a tie."

Thus supplied with a polka dot tie and plaid jacket that would have embarrassed a circus clown, Joel slid into the bar. There he spied a blonde crying into a martini.

"Oh *!!#%" she said.

"What's the matter?" he inquired.

"It's my *!!#@*% husband. I never see him, and we were to have drinks. I've been waiting for the lousy #!@* for an hour! He's spending all his time on the set, working on this lousy movie. It's always work, work, work. Well, @$$!#!"

She spoke as salty as a sailor. Fidgeting with a swizzle stick, Joel blushed at the way her pungent vocabulary contrasted with her flawless features, her peaches and cream skin.

"I think he's two timing me, the lousy !!!@&*."

"Love," he said with an expansive gesture, "is a four-letter word."

"Darn tootin'!"

Joel's elbow knocked over his own drink on the bar and it spilled over the edge of the bar and onto the actress' lap.

Joel mopped up the spill with a million napkins and felt her thighs though the sheer chiffon dress. She breathed more and more heavily. Meanwhile, the Brown Derby's cartoonist inked a drawing of the actress swooning and Joel at her feet. In five minutes Hedda Hopper, via the barman, had an item plastered all over the papers: *Guess what platinum-blond thesp is consorting with newcomer klutzy Casanova while he-man oater-star hubby stews in jealousy.*

Without lifting a finger, Joel, the loser's loser, was suddenly the most sought-after bachelor in Hollywood.

Joel Bartlett was jitterbugging with Joan Crawford at the Trocadero, cocktailing with Bette Davis at the Coconut Grove, and canoodling with a cigarette girl from Ciro's. And now he looked the part of a 30's roué as he exchanged his low-riding jeans for a fine chalkstripe suit with padded shoulders.

His fame as a lover and foot massager running apace, Joel was beginning to like it in the year 1938. Yes, indeed. He was invited in to do a screen test at MGM, then in the throes of making "The Wizard of Oz." While in the commissary, he was surrounded by an army of midgets who raised his self-esteem to the roof beams by making him taller than anybody else.

While there, he ran into Alicia, the potty-mouthed starlet with soft baby-blues he'd met at the Brown Derby. She spoke coyly, "Come to my dressing room when you get a chance."

One of the munchkins reached in Joel's pocket and grabbed Joel's Chronos Mark VII, the magical hand-held machine that linked him to the present. Squealing and laughing merrily, the tiny man danced a jig and pressed all the buttons with glee. Poof!—with a bit of twinkling dust the midget vanished. Joel gulped.

"Are you all right?" Alicia asked.

"Fine," he lied. Along with the midget, Joel's means to return to the present had vanished.

"Let's visit my dressing room," Alicia cooed. "Away from prying eyes and ears," and she tugged on his hand.

Once in the privacy of her dressing room, she shouted, "You ***&#@!!" and pummeled him with a silk pillow. "You've been romantically linked to Bette Davis and Eleanor Roosevelt. What have those *!!#@*! &*!!*#% got that I haven't got?"

"A cleaner mouth—"

"I don't know about that Roosevelt *&#@, but Bette can cuss with the best."

"I didn't mean cleaner in a metaphorical sense," Joel said. "They use mouth wash."

As if on cue, Jasper Wyoming, Alicia's jealous husband, burst in the door, and roared, "I caught you two together."

He fired off a several rounds from a shakily held pistol. The smell of burnt fireworks filled the room. Jasper was a poorer shot in real life than in the cowboy movies: with the bullets he'd managed to riddle the stucco. Joel ran outside the dressing room, and collided with a midget who suddenly materialized from thin air. Both landed on their backs.

Each leapt for the Chronos Mark VII. Joel managed to pry it from the munchkin and punched the red escape button, as the little man squeezed his tiny arms around Joel's knees.

Joel closed his eyes, and when he reopened them there were gleaming new cars and billboards for the latest movie. He was back where he belonged. For the first time in many days, his hand automatically reached for his cell phone, hidden in his vest pocket, and started playing back messages:

Monday 10:27 a.m. This is Sid. The producer at CBS still loves your first audition and wants you to go back and read for the neighbor with Tourette's syndrome. Oh yes, I've decided to be your agent again.

Monday 10:38 a.m. Where are you? Have you fallen off the face of the planet? This is Sid. We're looking for you like crazy. A call-back is in half an hour. Spielberg's people saw your headshots, and are interested in you for a supporting role in an unannounced project.

Monday 3:12 p.m. This is Shelly. To be honest, I was heart-broken when you forgot to call me on my birthday. I think we need some time apart to think over our relationship. . ."

Shelly's birthday was last month! He remembered the cell-phone salesman's warning, "The time you use when you go back into the past, will be used up on this end in future." Joel groaned and prepared to drop-kick the Chronos Mark VII tele-transporter from here to kingdom come.

Then he felt a tugging at his knee and heard a tiny munchkin voice:

"Give it to me. On my first trip to the future I discovered you can make like a bandit, taking pictures with the tourists in front of the Chinese theater. I can work here on the weekends and commute to 1938."

Joel gave the tele-transporter to the munchkin with his blessing. He had seen quite enough of the past.

Cute Kid

"Cute kid!" was not a phrase to naturally cross any-body's mind in regard to Kim's daughter. Karen should know: she had been an assistant to a casting director until the day before, when she got notice. Now as Karen and her friend Kim strolled the midway in the Oxnard Strawberry Festival, an earnest woman came up to the ugly girl with a balloon, and said, "What a cute kid. Kinda early Brooke Shields meets Drew Barrymore. Lotta personality. That X-factor," and facing Kim and Karen: "Which of you is the mother?"

Kim beamed with motherly pride. Then the little girl with a feral squirrel-like movement, turned her head and chomped her razor-sharp incisors into the sycophant's index finger. The woman moaned in terrific pain, yet heroically managed a final modulated, "Cute kid," as her firm but gentle hands quickly built distance between herself and the little monster.

Now her mother's friend Kim thought, lady, do you need your eyes examined? The child in question was flame-red haired, freckled with a lazy eye that wandered to the side without permission, big ears that stuck out like elves in the Mojave Desert. Most of her front teeth were owned by the tooth fairy and a plurality owned by tooth decay. A double rill of mucilage ran down under her nose on a permanent basis—only it wasn't mucilage. Her rust-colored hair resembled a Brillo pad, and her mother sometimes used the little gamine to scrub stubborn baked-on grime off pots and pans.

"She can be a star!" said the woman, still smarting from the bite. "What's her name?"

"Mildred. . ."

"Mildred. . . Mildred," she tasted it like a sample of a new ice-cream flavor. "It's so retro. I like it. After dear little Mildred is a superstar, there'll be a slew of Mildreds bopping around." An aside: "Do you think I should get a rabies shot?. . . Here's my card."

Kim glanced down and saw that it invited her to a special private audition at a Rodeo Drive address with Mr. Larry Mildew, "one of Hollywood's Top Children's Talent Agents." Needless to say, Mildred's mom was impressed.

The next day Kim stood in line with two hundred other children and expectant parents. The audition turned out to be on Rodeo Drive, all right, but the one in Baldwin Hills, not Beverly Hills. They were invited to fill out paperwork with their name, social security number, yearly income and DNA code. When facing questions from critical dads it was dismissed as, "standard show business procedure."

One family made a fuss and walked out, crying child in tow. "I wanna screen test, I wanna screen test," the child whined. The brusque departure made those who stayed behind feel smart and exclusive, even a little smug.

After completing the paperwork, Kim and Karen and little Mildred were handed a sample script to practice. Meanwhile they waited for one group of parents and child hopefuls to vacate the room where the Mildew Agency made its presentation. Each time a new group would occupy the still-warm plush seats, those in the hallway would advance a few yards, and pause under giant blow-up photos placed at intervals; now Shirley Temple, now, Macaulay Culkin, now Robert Blake. The script they were handed could already be heard ad infinitum as one mother practiced with her daughter.

"I want you to be natural," the mother was saying. "Just be yourself."

The child gave a listless line reading, "I went to the dentist," she opened her mouth. "And look, ma, no cavities."

The original dialogue had an exclamation on the end.

"No, Angelica," her mom said, "Do it like this. . ." And the mom proceeded to restore two exclamations to the line. The daughter read the line a second time, if anything a more listless rendition.

"Like this," mom got tense around the neck and shoulders. "I went to the dentist. And look, ma, no cavities!"

The child got halfway through the line and started playing toesy. The mother yanked on a ponytail and said, "Angelica, you're gonna get this line right if it's the last thing you do. . . Now just be yourself."

Karen, the former casting assistant, turned to her friend Kim and said, "I don't know if you're cut out to be a stage mother. You seem pretty lax, Kim."

When finally they were disgorged into a screening room and Mr. Mildew was introduced.

Karen's hackles were up from the moment people were asked for their annual income on the application. She smelled a rat in here somewhere, a rat named Larry K. Mildew, head of the children's talent agency. The minute she got home she'd IMDB him.

All the hopeful parents and their progeny sat in comfortable plush theater chairs and stared at an empty screen. Mildred, Mildred's mother, and her mother's best friend—recently unemployed Karen—sat expectantly.

In the background you could hear the one mother still coaching her child, "No Deisha, that was blasé. Put some zip into your voice! Deisha, like this," flinging her arms skyward, "Look ma, no cavities!"

The stagestruck mother performed her line with the gusto of a kid on a Halloween sugar high. A rumpled man took a live mike, occasioning a loud thump that left half the crowd needing to schedule appointments with an ear specialist.

"Ladies and gentlemen, we're not looking for the next Britney Spears, River Phoenix or Leslie Nielsen." The parents were so ravenous for fame and residuals that none noticed Leslie Nielsen wasn't even a child actor. "We just want kids who are kids. Kids who wanna have fun and consume sugar. And all of this should be fun for kids and parents. I speak from experience," said the man, "I'm Larry K. Mildew."

The man seemed to be a child trapped inside a sagging middle-aged body. A sandy mullet dropped down below his collar. He jumped and twirled around the podium with the energy of an Olympic Tri-athlete, doing curlicues with the microphone in his hand. "I had my first bowel movement on 'Golden Girls,' my first kiss on 'Punky Brewster,' my first STD on 'Full House' with the Olsen twins—and I was only three years old! That child actor's life, riding a tricycle in the fast lane, is no bed of roses. No sir. And my parents, with their clever accountant found ways to siphon money off my Jackie Coogan account—you'll learn more about that—and spent nights on the town while they overdosed me on pediatric cough syrup and locked me in a closet. Lemme tell you, that stuff put me into therapy for 50 years and I'm only 39 years old—go figure."

Mr. Mildew put his head down on the podium and wept. After a minute he struggled again to speak:

"Because of my pain, I live to see that each and every child actor is rewarded with utmost respect and humane treatment."

"And don't forget the residuals!" heckled the stage mom.

Karen, the former casting agent assistant, watched it all with a jaded eye, as finally the children were called up one by one to do their test. Their innocent faces were projected onto the large screen. Little Mildred spoke in a low inaudible voice and swallowed her lines. The audience couldn't have discerned if she was pitching tooth paste or Viagra. Her performance was greeted by polite but muted applause. Meanwhile, the girl who had been relentlessly coached did a superb job, striking a balance between clarity and goofy childhood exuberance. Shirley Temple couldn't have done it better, and yet, after the applause petered out, from behind the last aisle of plush seats, came the cruel sound of a maternal hand applied smartly to buttocks and the child's heartbreaking squall pursued everyone's ears.

"I told you to do it with *feeling*," the mom snapped. "That sounded like death warmed over."

Mr. Mildew returned at the end, somewhat recomposed with his mullet toupee askew, and told the audience that only the top twenty most talented children would be chosen for 'development' by his agency. Mildew sowed high drama, for dozens of children had responded to the cattle call.

"As you exit," Mildew said, "stop at the table with my associates to turn in your application form."

Kim, Mildred's mother, was smitten as they exited the theater.

"Did you see Mildred up there. She's fantastic."

Meanwhile, little Mildred said, "I wasn't fantastic, I was fabulous. . . Now I want ice cream. And none of the cheap Rite Aid crap, either."

Kim, Karen and Mildred waited in line. Fortune had placed them right in front of the stage mother. Karen said how talented she thought her daughter Deisha was. The stage mother flushed with pride at these words. Karen got her phone number with the promise of her casting-agent connections. In fact, Karen was doing some detective work; what she really intended was to get the results of talented Deisha's audition and compare them to homely Mildred's. It was criminal how these people trafficked in kids' and parents' Hollywood hopes.

When Mildred sat down in front of Mr. Mildew's 'associate,' the woman asked for the business card they had received at the Oxnard Stawberry Festival. There ensued a neurotic search through pockets and handbags. Karen asked, "Why do you need the card?"

"The associate who discovered your daughter, has their employee code," she replied. "They will get their commission for the find. Now," the woman turned to Kim,

Mildred's mother. "We will call you within three days. Only the top twenty most talented children will be chosen to work with Mr. Mildew. Good luck!"

"Hello this is Miss Thalamus, secretary at the Mildew Agency. Please hold for Mr. Mildew. . ."

The call came the next morning—not even a full 24-hours had passed. Kim was in raptures, she was going to get to talk to the fellow who headed the whole shebang, the accomplished former child actor, who'd poured out his heart at the audition and brought a roomful of would-be stage parents to tears.

Showing histrionic mastery, Mildew kept her on the edge of her seat, explaining, "We looked at little Mildred's tape, and she's got a lot of promise." Right away Kim braced herself for disappointment: promise is not one of those words that are promising, rather they are pulled out to soften the blow. "There are three basic responses: yes, no and maybe. Then there are four sub-categories: no-no, the no-maybe, the yes-yes, and the yes-maybe. 'No-no' means no way, the kid doesn't have the aptitude, forgets lines, oughta be playing baseball; 'no-maybe' is something there, come back in six months, maybe they'll be ready." Though she was flattered how much time such a busy and important show business figure as Mr. Mildew was dedicating to her, Kim devoutly wished he'd cut the chase and get to the point. "'Yes-yes,' is we'll sign the child up and send 'em out on some auditions right off the bat. Mildred is a. . . Oh, sorry, could you hold just a moment?"

Kim cupped the phone and shouted, "Karen! It's Mr. Mildew on the line, the head honcho of the children's agency." Karen, the unemployed casting agent assistant, recently ejected from a studio apartment on Hawthorne Ave., was now sleeping on Kim's couch.

After a few seconds Mildew came back on the line: "I'm so sorry to interrupt. That was Spielberg calling. Now what was I saying? Mildred, yes. We've seen her audition tape and she's a definite yes-maybe. We think she's really got something original. She needs some classes, though, before she's audition-ready. And this is the big time; you don't want a talent like Mildred going out and blowing the chances for the rest of her career. I'd like to meet you halfway. I'll get the headshots for Mildred and you sign her up for acting and elocution classes."

Kim hung up ecstatic. "They chose Mildred! She was in the top twenty!"

"Kim, can't you see?" said Karen. "They're setting you up, saying she's not ready. They'll have Mildred in acting and dancing classes longer than Freud was in therapy."

"Who's Freud?"

Karen's face fell like a TV set thrown out of the Sunset Hyatt.

"To tell you the truth," Karen said, "I was hoping they wouldn't choose Mildred."

"You're saying she has no talent?" Mildred's mom said.

"No no no. In my spare time I've been looking up Mildew. It ain't pretty, and I was hoping I wouldn't have to share this with you. He's never been child actor. And he's wanted in Alabama for setting mileage back on used ice-cream trucks."

"Everybody can turn over a new leaf," said Kim. "Besides, Mildred has talent. He said so."

Undeterred, Kim signed her homely daughter up for the acting classes. The classes were being held after school on Wednesdays at a vacant office on Wilshire Boulevard. After the third week, Kim became slightly suspicious of Mildew

Enterprises when nobody ever appeared to give the class. That, and the fact that her bank account had been pretty well vacuumed out via her routing number, prompted some serious reflection.

"What the hell am I going to do?" Kim exclaimed to her friend Karen. "There are bills due and the refrigerator is bare. I need to buy reverse osmosis water and chocolate with 70% cacao content."

"I've got an idea," Karen said with quiet cunning. "There's nothing easier than conning a conner. But we're gonna need Mildred's thespian chops to pull this off."

The erstwhile casting agent assistant signed as a headhunter for the Mildew Children's Agency and traveled all the fairs and festivals where children were likely to congregate. It was a blast: she got to go to Disneyland, Knotts' Berry Farm, holiday parades, the Santa Monica pier, toy stores and circuses. Her come on, regardless of whether the youngster had a mug like Lillian Hellman, was:

"What a cute kid! Your son (or daughter) could be in movies."

Pug-faced Mildred, who certainly looked as if somebody had pasted Lillian Hellman's face on a child's body, was Karen's first guinea pig in her plot against the Mildew Children's Talent Agency. She dressed her in cute little Texas boots, a tasseled skirt, cowhide-patterned vest and cowboy hat, toy six-shooters slapping Mildred's little thighs.

As a former assistant to a casting agent, she planned scrupulously for every 'contingency' (industry lingo for glitch). For her inaugural scam she took no chances that the parents of returning auditions be recognized by the Mildew staff. She contacted, Deisha's mom, the stage mother, and did a switcheroo. Mildred's mom played Deisha's mom, Deisha's mom played Mildred's mom.

If one of Mildew's registration lackeys asked why Mildred was white and her mom was Eurasian, she would say that Mildred had been adopted. When the moment of truth came, the registering clerk, Mildew's lackey, didn't even bat an eyelash. Karen promptly received two commissions (for Deisha and Mildred), and kicked back a tidy sum to the mothers for their trouble. Emboldened by their lackadaisical approach, Karen decided the following week to give the girls brand-new disguises and be accompanied by their actual moms. It worked like a charm—two more commissions.

Now Karen went all out and started forming a network of mothers and auditioning children from an ever growing pool. There were parents who actually signed up for the acting and singing and tap-dancing lessons at the non-existent Mildew Academy, and they were fighting mad after getting bilked. Karen got her strongest participants from that group who saw through the sham from the start. She could offer genuine 'acting experience' to put on their child's resume as they impersonated different children and features.

Karen had perfected dozens of disguises, using both wardrobe and prosthetics, and the kids loved getting dressed and made up. One week it was cowgirl, the next geisha, the next kung-fu kid, the next hippie love child with tie-die shirt and a feather in their hair, smartly dressed Gap children and begrimed trailer-trash tykes. Kim, Mildred's mother was adept at helping Karen so the costuming and clothing fell into place.

In a few weeks she had her own parasitic industry, under the name "Kids of 1000 Faces." She was charging parents a sign-up fee, and Karen was also getting bonuses from the Mildew Agency for each child she brought in. This money became a magnet for new parents signing up, and it was vital for keeping a roof over their heads, as Kim, Mildred's mom, continued to lose a bundle on acting and singing lessons for her daughter whom she was taking to other agencies belonging to the same ilk as Mildew Enterprises. There was a silver lining, however: as Mildred's mom, Kim, went further astray and into debt, Karen discovered a small galaxy of agencies that followed the same fraudulent modus operandi as Mr. Mildew, and she realized "Kids of 1000 Faces" was ripe to expand.

Mildred had always been her prototype for the disguises, leading the way for the stable of children. The challenge came when she ran out of costume ideas for Mildred. After supervising hundreds of clever disguises, the possibilities— except colored contact lenses and changing skin pigmentation—had been exhausted. All the group's forty other children were staggered behind Mildred, but they would soon be due for a change in the weeks ahead, and Karen was running out of ideas.

Crisis! It seemed Karen's elaborate scam to pass off the same children as new finds for the fraudulent Mildew Talent Agency was reaching the end of the trail.

"Midgets," Karen burst out.

"What?" said Kim.

"We start from scratch and begin recruiting midgets."

Kim said, "Don't call them midgets, they're little actors. You should know that; you're the one with industry experience. And Karen, if you're asking for my opinion, I think it's a lousy idea."

At mention of the word 'lousy' all the vermin massing and multiplying in six-year-old Mildred's Brillo-like hair, stood at reveille.

With a sandpaper sound, Mildred itched behind her ears, on the top of her head, and in the curve of her neck. The scratching had been going on for some time now, but Kim and Karen had been too immersed in "Kids of 1000 Faces," to take note. Now Karen gaped as her fingers exposed a lively infestation in Mildred's hair.

"We always thought it would be nice to have a small pet," said Mildred's horrified mom. "But not this small."

After a week of combing out white nits with a fine-toothed comb, and shampooing with liquid that would have set off a Geiger counter, the colony of lice continued to colonize. Kim, as Mildred's mom, decided the best way to deal with the infestation was shaving off Mildred's hair. At first Karen was furious.

"Everyone will think she's a boy," she snapped. "And she'll be traumatized. You oughta be nailed for child abuse."

"Look who's talking! You're milking a scheme to get commissions from all the fake children's talent agencies."

Karen had an idea: "Mildred. . . we could change her name to Millard. We'll be getting commissions for yet another person. I think she'd look cute in lederhosen. In fact Mildred may look better as a boy."

As Mildred became acutely aware of, and self-conscious about the tonsorial change, she started wrapping her buzzed head in a purple bandanna.

It was then, after Mildred's radical haircut, that Karen noticed another change. People. would stare at Mildred compassionately. Folks on the street began to spontaneously give the beauty-challenged child candy, silver and copper coins, and toys, and tickets to Disneyland, and to gaze at Mildred with uncommon sympathy. Mildred's mother chalked it up to Mildred's surfeit of natural charm and charisma.

One lady, after handing Mildred an Xbox, hesitatingly asked, "I hope she's going to be all right."

"Yes," Kim replied. Yes seemed like the thing to say, and then she asked, "What do you mean?"

"Is she well?" inquired the woman.

"Of course I'm well," Mildred spat out, tiny saliva projectiles emitting from her wide mouth.

"She's not on chemo?"

"On chemo? Oh no," Kim laughed. "She's perfectly fine."

"Are you sure," the lady asked.

"Sure I'm sure," replied Kim.

"In that case I'll take back my Xbox."

Karen and Kim saw this month's rent dissolve before their eyes.

"She's well in terms of spirits," Karen chimed in. "Oh, she's beyond chemo. At stage 4 pulmonary melanoma."

"That's right," Kim spoke up and dropped the Xbox into her handbag.

Mildred's mom learned to shut her trap and the gifts flowed. It explained why people spontaneously knitted caps for her. Why they gave her ice-cream cones and daisies. Why their smiles were accentuated by a tearful glaze. Her mom even heightened the sickly look, putting purplish shadow below her eyes and increasing sallowness in her cheeks, while coaching Mildred on the nuances of a bronchial cough. Mildred got far more bank when she was taken to be a sick child than she ever got from the Mildew Agency.

It took about two minutes for Karen to decide to convene the whole "Kids of 1000 Faces" group and propose shaving them all.

For some parents that was too much. They greeted the proposition with a turned back and accusations of cruelty, but those troupers who stayed were soon reaping the rewards like an early bird in a well-oiled Ponzi scheme, raking in donations and sympathy. They were providing a valuable service to the donors: giving them the priceless experience of contributing. Indeed, "Kids of 1000 Faces" had become a factory for Samaritans. Who's to say there wasn't a speck of charity in the heartless heart of Karen's scam and in that speck a universe of love?

The world was a bit happier thanks to Karen's scheme. A few more families could put ham, tofu *and* turkey on the holiday table and toys under the Hanukkah tree. Mildred still bit a few Samaritans' noses, and still people would peer down at her and say, "Cute kid," lying through their teeth.

Daylock

A wave of tension broke and washed over me the moment I stepped into the room. The tension crackled in the air and raised the hairs on my forearms. I wasn't used to this kind of reception. Me, a pencil-neck computer geek with a plastic pen liner in my shirt pocket.

George, pooh-bah of the Hollywood Six, sat on the broken-backed office chair, over the broken patch of plastic carpet mat, and nervously folded his soft pink hands over his ample paunch, girded in white broadcloth splotched here and there by tiny Rorschach blots of melted butter. Then, with the devious smile of a child, fully aware he's doing something wrong, George succumbed to the temptation of popcorn from a Dixie cup on the box office desk. He knew darn well what that stuff did to his cholesterol and his waistline.

"Six suspects six—one for each house of the movie theater," George quipped and let out a sickly, nervous laugh. "There was the Secaucus Seven. We're the Hollywood Six."

George's globe-shaped head, crowned by a jet-black toupee, made of a shiny material somewhat less pliant than fiberglass, was on the chopping block. As operations chief for our little family-owned theater chain, I had driven from Santa Monica to investigate a series of thefts that had shook up the Hollywood Six. Now, after collecting written statements from all the employees and interviewing them one by one, in the dark recesses of the projection booth during the last two days, I was ready to announce my findings.

Theft number one occurred only days after I taped a sign on the safe, saying, "Do Not Leave in Daylock." I had noticed them doing this—leaving the safe door closed and the combination open—and it's an invitation to trouble, even if it's a real timesaver for managers, who throughout the day are called upon to replenish the cashiers' supply of bills. The managers at the Hollywood Six often left the safe door ajar, so they could get in at a tug of a handle, instead of having to spin the numbered dial so many times left and right until hearing the audible click. True, nobody at the Hollywood Six had ever lost any serious money, but we were soon to install surveillance cameras in the box office, and I put up the daylock warning as a cautionary measure. In retrospect, I see it as an omen of troubles ahead. Within the week, eight hundred dollars in crisp new banded stacks vanished from the safe. Just like that.

Eight-hundred dollars isn't enough money to skip to Mexico on, but it shattered our trust. And just as things seemed to settle down and return to normal, the thief struck again. The second theft was less in amount—a mere two hundred dollars—and greater in impact: it unleashed a rampant distrust and thrillride sensation. When would the thief strike again? A dizziness now mingled with the popcorn smell in the air. I had seen it before at other theaters, when a theft occurs, the whole atmosphere is taken over by loosey goosey feeling between curiosity and disbelief. The locomotive has jumped the tracks, the train cars speed out of control, and you can only wait in mute agony for the crash.

I asked everyone to e-mail me a thorough account of their movements that day of the first robbery. George, the head manager, wrote back immediately, and Jeff, recently promoted from floor staff to manager. Nathan, the night manager, for some reason unknown to me, never troubled to e-mail.

Statement by Jeff, Assistant Manager of the Hollywood Six

"The afternoon the money disappeared, I close out the box a little early, just after 5 p.m. It had been a slow Thursday afternoon, so I takes advantage of the lull to close out the registers in the candy concession. Leaving Ashley in the box, I left the safe in daylock. A few minutes later I returned to the box with the money picked up from the registers in the clipboard. In the box, Ashley was already visiting with Jared, who had just dropped by for a visit. He wasn't selling tickets. At around 5:20 I set out to do a deposit, and a customer come up to the ticket window with a hundred dollar bill. Since there was no twenties in the drawer, I had to get some money from the safe. I give Ashley 200 in fives. At that time I was 100% sure all the money was there, 800 in five dollar bills. One thing I'm not sure about, tho, is if the safe door was locked or open. I have to be honest.

"Around 6 p.m. Peggy come scratching on the box door—you always know it's her by that cat scratch on the door. Peggy had crossed Ashley on her way out the bathroom. Around that time I remember the cleaning lady, coming in to empty the wastebasket. George come in about 5:30. From the box office window, I seen him walking around the front of the theater. I lowered the tall curtain over the desk and safe: he always considers this unsightly for the customers and gripes about the curtain not being down. If you have any questions, sir, I am at your service."

Statement by George, Head Manager of the Hollywood Six

"I was actually the first person to discover the missing money, though I didn't recognize it as a theft at the time. After I arrived, Andres, one of the 'popcorn pushers' told me that one of the johns in the men's room was running over, and I hurried off to take care of it. A few minutes after 6, after Jared (the employee) finished his visit with Peggy and left the box. I then entered the box. Peggy asked for 300 in singles for change. I opened the safe and took out the packs of banded 100's and noticed we were completely out of fives. I thought nothing of it because the change order—a batch of fresh fives and singles—was due the next day. I gave Peggy the packs of singles and closed the safe door, leaving it unlocked.

"Not until 8:30 when the assistant night manager, Nathan, made the deposit drop did he notice the missing bills—there were no five-dollar bills. He immediately checked the safe count from the 6:00 p.m. closing and shift change. Nathan called Jeff, and he came in his jogging clothes to see if I could find the money. To see if it had been set on a shelf or been misplaced."

Head Manager George completed his statement, saying, "Robberies happen at other sloppy theaters, but not the Hollywood Six."

Three days after George asserted that "Robberies happen at other sloppy theaters, but not the Hollywood Six," the thief (or thieves) struck again. At night two hundred dollars was missing from the ticket box sales. The same cast was involved. Jared, the musician, was on the night shift, Ashley had been on the day shift. Jared neglected to count the drawer when the shift started—that's the one loophole that could admit his guilt.

Two robberies in the space of one week. Enough was enough, and the old man had me drive to Sunset Strip in person.

Upstairs in the projection booth, as movies unspooled in the darkness, I interviewed Ashley, who'd been selling tickets during the first robbery. She swore up and down she was in the box office the whole time, visiting Jared. Jared likewise maintained he had been in the box the whole time visiting Ashley. If anybody had opened the safe, they would have seen each other. Only the managers knew the combination to the safe, Ashley said, but I pointed out that a box person could have observed the combination over time.

Ashley's and Jared's statements both corroborated that they had spent that crucial thirty-five minutes from 5:20 to 5:55 together in the box office, talking, that slow Thursday afternoon. The only variation between the two accounts was

Jared's mention that he "turned briefly to the open hatch between the concession and the box office to be handed a diet Coke by Andres." Andres stated that Ashley, to the best of his knowledge, stood at the ticket window the whole time.

I talked to George and Juana, the cleaning lady, as well as Nathan and Jeff, the two assistant managers. The only English Juana knew besides good morning and good bye was "yes." If I had asked her if she'd stolen the money, she would have nodded gravely and said "ye-es." If I had asked her if she had stolen twenty million dollars, she would have nodded gravely and said "ye-es." Other than that, everyone seemed to support each other's stories, and nobody fell into any glaring contradictions.

I thought about this as I drove through tedious traffic back to Santa Monica, and thought about how Jeff had provided a detailed, too detailed, account of his movements the night of the first robbery.

At home, Sam and Jenny were in bed, and my wife waited with cold lasagna. We talked about the case as it was shaping up. There was something fascinating and also maddening about it, because it should have been so easy to solve, a no-brainer. Consider the elements: an Agatha Christie set-up, a completely enclosed space, the box office—one entrance and exit—and a limited number of suspects.

"Melvin," my wife asked. "What are these people like?"

"You mean the suspects?" I said, falling into police jargon. Marsha nodded yes. "Jeff is very clean-cut, straight arrow, bad grammar. He's a country boy. Out from Mississippi to pursue the Hollywood dream. George, you know George from the employee Christmas party."

"Does he still have that awful toupee?" she said from the kitchen sink.

"Nathan, assistant manager, young guy in his twenties, wears an earring. Ashley is the box office girl. Chews gum." I left out dishwater blond. Marsha knows how I feel about dishwater blonds. "Jared, the box office guy, is kind of shifty, unshaven. The Seattle grunge type."

"Who has a motive?" Joanna asked.

"Hmn. . . I was much more concerned about their movements the day of the robbery. Just the facts should speak for themselves."

"You're talking like Joe Friday," Joanna said. "What about motives."

"Motives, huh?"

"Old George is an incurable gossip, you must have heard something," Marsha said, moving the oversize spoon in the lasagna and giving me another helping.

Hearing my wife's questions, I at once realized that the interviews had been the least important part of my visit to the Hollywood Six; everything else people were saying and doing around me—things I had dismissed as subjective and circumstantial—were what mattered. Like what I had heard eaves-dropping on the step behind the burgundy curtain in the box office as George and Peggy Mulholland blabbed.

"I heard Jared's van had broken down, his roommate was moving out, and he ended his band tour early. Peggy said he's also been dreading the arrival of surveillance cameras. Big Brother. 'If anyone if going to rob. Now's the time to do it.' He said this to Ashley more as a joke. That's how they took it. Ashley may have her motives, too. George says she has been under extreme emotional stress. Her aunt had a terminal illness and she needed one thousand dollars to hire a voodoo priestess. In the last two weeks he's seen her in tears at the beginning of her shift. According to Peggy,

Ashley is a real party girl and she's generous with the back rubs. Especially with Nathan, who is quite taken with her."

"Maybe she thinks by spreading the sugar she can get away with murder," Marsha remarked.

"Peggy thinks the thousand dollars went up Ashley's nose," I said as I took the dirtied dishes from the kitchen table.

"What does George say about who did it?" Marsha said. "Anybody as unsubtle as him must have an opinion."

"It's Ashley all the way. He says the bitch did it. But anybody so brazen as to do this robbery is going to lose their job, and, according to everybody, Ashley loves her job. Jeff, the other manager, says it seemed unlikely that she'd have opened the safe and scooped out the packs of bills, risk him walking back any time and capturing her in the act."

"Is George himself ruled out as a suspect?" Marsha asked.

"Not entirely. Nate, the assistant manager on the night shift, told me that when he questioned George about whether there had been fives in the safe, he answered immediately, without hesitation, that there had been no fives. Usually he has to stammer and think about things. Actually Nate said George has been complaining about trouble making his mortgage payments, and he's been padding his hours on the job. Coming early and slipping into a movie. What do you think, Marsha? What does your intuition tell you about this case?"

"It's always the one you least suspect."

In tribute to the goodness of the people they worked with, the employees of the Hollywood Six still held out hope that it was all a mistake, a shitty mistake, that the money had been dropped on the side of the safe or mistakenly gone into the deposit. Money, though, is something that never gets misplaced, it just gets into different hands.

Coming down the steps into the box office, after six hours of interviews, I cleared my throat and said:

"I'm about to announce the results of our in-house investigation."

There was a pause and all faces turned to me. George coughed an excuse to go get some popcorn upstairs. At a time like this you'd think he would have thought of something other than popcorn. He lumbered up from the chair and stepped outside. We waited. Fanning our hands in the heat of the summer night.

"Criminy," Peggy said.

"I'm going to wait till he gets back," I said.

We all sat in the stifling heat of the box office. It's amazing you could fit so many grown people into the cramped space. Peggy Mulholland sat at the open box window, smudged by the paws of many moviegoers, fanning herself with a half-finished crossword. Jared leaned on the counting table, where he'd been leaning the day the crimes started. He stared out shiftily from under his auburn bangs. I saw the shadows under his and Nathan's eyes, so I knew I wasn't the only one losing sleep over this. Ashley sat on a folding chair, arms and legs crossed. Dishwater blond, chewing gum and legs from here to Kansas City. Juana, up in the shadows at the top of the stairs, by the door to the theater lobby, had a feather duster in her hand and seemed to resist moving it toward the dandruff on Jared's shoulders.

"I wonder what's taking George so long," muttered Peggy.

"I'll take a look," Jared offered.

I studied the walls. What a dump the box office was considering how much money came through this place. Sunfaded crimson curtains hung down, tattered, hiding the unsightly stairs and manager's desk and computer. The rancid reek of too much fast food clung to the walls and carpet, sticky from spilled soda. Boxes of sweaty employee shirts lay jumbled at the foot of the stair. The drab muscatel-colored paint was specked where scotch tape had torn it and spattered by dried cola. A good weekend and a couple blockbusters on screen one and six, the big houses, the Hollywood Six would rake in fifty thousand. If somebody really wanted to rob this place. . .

Jared came to the door and panted out, "George's sprawled out on the floor by the back door."

"What?" Ashley asked in a bitchy, can't-be-bothered tone.

"Somebody call 911."

George lay supine on the floor, popcorn kernels fanned out from a small cup, stuck to the floor with double butter. A thread of drool came out of the corner of his meaty lips. His jet-black toupee had fallen off his head and onto the floor. Peggy wadded up one of the dirty employee shirts and put it under George's head for comfort, but on her way over she'd stepped on the fallen toupe and it made a crackling sound like a cockroach stomped on.

An ambulance was called, and George was whisked away. I left without making my announcement. My mind was a shambles, my conclusions in jeopardy. I said, "I'm gonna have to go back to Santa Monica and discuss this with Jerry." Jerry was the bearded old man, the owner of the chain. "We'll have a determination by the end of the week."

I said it like I meant it.

George was in the hospital for a week, recovering from a triple bypass. George's nemesis had been popcorn and hydrogenated popcorn butter, but that didn't stop speculation that he had been the victim of foul play. To top it all off, the theater was robbed a third time.

It happened just as I drove in to check up on the Hollywood Six and see how the new security measures were going at the Hollywood Six.

This time shared one great similarity with the first theft: it occurred at the shift change. A time of people coming and going, confusion, the right hand not knowing what the left held. Jeff got Ashley's pick-up from the box-office drawer and Vegas box. She counted it; he double counted it. He went upstairs to collect cash from the concession registers and left the box money on the desk—a fact Jeff said he regretted because Ashley was one of the prime suspects. Two 500-packs of 20's and $120 in loose twenties. When Jeff picked up the top pack the clip came off and I recounted the five-dollar bills. One hundred were missing in fives and one hundred in loose twenties.

"Oh, shit," Jeff muttered under his breath just as I stepped into the box office.

"What did you say?" I asked.

"Melvin, I think we're short again," he said.

Nathan trudged in for the night shift. Peggy arrived too and Nate told her to wait upstairs until we had sorted this out. Ashley was upset, chewed her gum more furiously, tears came to her eyes. "What did I do? Where's the money?"

She offered to take her clothes off. Nobody was stopping her, though in my official capacity I had to say something.

"You don't have to do that," I told her.

Ashley had already stripped down to her skivvies, she took off her bra and offered to take off more. Poured out all the junk from her backpack. She was very, very upset. As Nate said, "If she really did it, and lied to us, she deserves an Academy Award." Or at least a Golden Globe, I thought.

She had been thoroughly searched, there was no way she could have gotten out of the building with the money.

"Where was Jared?" my wife asked at home.

"At the time of the third theft, Jared had been talking at the box window to Ashley."

"This guy has a knack for being at the wrong place," Marsha observed.

"Of course Ashley didn't have the money on her person."

"She could have slipped it out of the slot for change and tickets, slipped it to him. They could have been in it together," Marsha said.

"You're smart, Marsha. That's why I married you."

"If I was that smart, why did I marry you?" Marsha retorted. There was a foxy glint in her eyes.

"What looks bad is Jared's end-of-shift departure, just about to leave when talking at the window to Ashley."

"You know, I have a theory that one person committed the first robbery and the others were copycats. It's only a theory."

"The only ones definitely in the clear are George and Juana, who'd had come in the box office to empty the garbage the night of the first robbery. She'd come in and out and was never left alone for a minute."

"Whoever it is is just getting more brazen," my wife said. "They're going to get overconfident and trip themselves up."

For a fact, I can tell you that the old man wanted to can everyone involved, including George. I fought tooth and nail for Nathan and Jeff, the assistant managers. They were spared. Then came the bombshell: Ashley and Jared were fired. I'm the one who did the firing, of course. It was the sacrifice, to get all this behind us. People at the bottom of the ladder always suffer. It bothers me, and yet I have a job to do. That still doesn't mean I didn't take a lot of shit for firing Jared. Even one of the popcorn pushers tried to chew me out, convinced he's a good guy, good as gold.

"But," I tried to tell them, "there's no way to prove Jared is innocent."

There was no real closure, no satisfaction of knowing who really did it.

That's the difference between real crime and Agatha Christie. There's a neat tidy ending, a sense of the proper punishment. At the Hollywood Six there was a lingering malaise. The guilt hung thick in the air.

Marsha wasn't at all pleased. She insisted that we had cleaned out the wrong people.

"You're no Sherlock Holmes, Melvin," she said.

"At least the robberies have stopped."

"Du-uh. You installed surveillance cameras."

Thanks to the cameras I can sit in my office in West L.A. and bring up the Hollywood Six on the computer screen. George, pooh-bah of the Six, is back, propped up at the door, taking tickets. After surgery he is ghastly thin, the blue blazer falls loosely around his once butterball belly. "Hi, howya doing?" rip. "Hi, howya doing?" rip. Getting sloppy, he neglects to drop it into the slot, the stubs flutter lamely to the floor. He has stopped donning the jet-black toupee, and I am reconciled to never knowing what really happened at the Hollywood Six.

Ashley, suspect number one, has a job as a waitress at Rocking Sushi in the mall. Whenever George sees Ashley sashay by the theater in her low-cut, spandex blouses, he damn near has an apoplectic seizure, convinced of her guilt. The anger inches one foot closer to the grave, and ready to join the foot that's already there. When other employees greet her, he hisses, "Don't talk to that lying minx on company time. . ."

That's the cruelty of this small stakes robbery, the suspect Ashley is still around to sprinkle some salt in a wound that won't heal. Not ever. Yes, eventually we will find out what happened. The truth comes out, but the truth cannot undo the murder of trust. It can only explain. So what if Ashley left the box office with the money grabbed when Jared wasn't looking? So what if she coolly crossed the theater lobby and stashed it in the ladies room cabinet where toilet paper and tampons were stored, the money tucked inside the toilet-paper spools, to be retrieved later in her backpack? There, are you happy? I'm not.

You know, most of us live our lives in daylock—the safe door is open, the goodies are inside for anybody to grab. Somebody comes along, does the dirty deed and then the padlocks go on, the guard is up, the shades go down. We become vulnerable as cheating husbands, foolish as drunken cockroaches, spineless as snails out of their shells. And every time it happens, we lose a little piece of our soul.

Capital Pains

"A few commentators have been concerned that
changes in estate tax provide incentives to change
the timing of death, a phenomenon termed 'death
elasticity.' Dr. George E. Mendenhall has warned
that large discontinuities in the estate tax rates, as
planned in 2010 and 2011, may provide incentives
to hasten death (late 2010) or prolong life (late
2009) for large financial implication."

Wikipedia, "Estate Tax in the United States"

Death Distracted

January 1, 2010. . . 12:01 a.m.

Jerry Klinger had had the sagacity to renounce the last
painful round of chemo, particularly since he was being
treated for social anxiety disorder, and fulfill a lifelong dream

of creating a scholarship fund for single, unwedded parrots. Now he gazed down from above and saw himself being worked over by an electric octopus of rubber-clad tentacles in the chamber where he had chosen to die—at home with dignity, surrounded by loved ones and familiar things: the throaty whirring of power lawn mowers, the weightiness of the Sunday Times, and the keen wailing of bagpipes.

Accompanied by a staple-gun sound, a spasm of current jolted the rubber octopus on Jerry's sunken chest, and his withered limbs, briefly animated, quivered and, just as quickly as they had come to life, fell deathly still.

Suddenly, like a kite broken and liberated from the string, Jerry felt free as a wind-bounced balloon. Heir to as many eyes as the northern wind has: now Jerry *was* the buffeting breeze, now the luminous light of the stars, which grew to a blinding intensity. Bliss overwhelmed the retired meat inspector, a bliss rarified and unalloyed, as he beheld Daphne, radiant against a sapphire shore. Her lavender eyes glowed, fine filaments of her hair blew in the silky breeze. Ageless, the features of Daphne, his late wife, embodied all her ages: the young woman on whose body he used to crayon the cuts of beef; the loving mother who used to crayon the cuts of beef on her children; the doting grandmother with a soft spot for bagpipe music. (The LP "Highland Pipes" had been the prelude to their most maniacal lovemaking, and the neighbors in their old apartment used to yell out the window, *Hey, did a policeman die in there?*)

"Jerry. . ." she sighed.

"Daphne. . ." he said.

A staple-gun sound intruded on their private Edenic tableau, then the flat, slightly nasal voice of Ryan Seacrest, narrating the New Year's revelry on Times Square. Jerry's crinkly eyelids opened wider that Alex's in *A Clockwork Orange*.

Jerry, restored to his wretched body, raved at the surrounding choir of medics and smiling relatives. "I saw the most fantastic world. And there was this bright bright light, and then Daphne appeared," he said hoarsely, pinioned by an overwhelming sense of loss. "Take me back!" he sobbed.

Medics hoisted the feeble man onto a stretcher, kicking and screaming.

Dementia, the family mouthed to medics. *Dementia*, they chanted.

"That's an out and out lie!" Jerry thundered from the stretcher.

Dementia, they explained to the medics, who gave the patient a potent sedative. The kicking limbs were soon becalmed.

"Sit tight, Jerry," his son-in-law said consolingly, before the ambulance doors closed on Jerry. "You're gonna be with us at least through the start of the fiscal new year. There could be a large financial implication involved."

911

OPERATOR: Hello, 911 Emergency.

CALLER: 911 emergency?

OPERATOR: Yes, that's right.

CALLER: Hey, is this 911 for sure?

OPERATOR: Yes.

CALLER: Are you *sure* this is 911? I've never called 911 before, and I'm very nervous. My hands are shaking. I'm nauseous. (*prolonged pause*) Are you still there? (*more silence*) You still there? Hello hello hello.

OPERATOR: Yes, I'm here.

CALLER: This is 911?

OPERATOR: Yes. (*angrily*) Now what's the emergency?

CALLER: (*sigh*) Where do I begin?

OPERATOR: Is there an emergency? You better hurry up. You can be prosecuted for wasting my time and blocking this line from somebody with a real emergency who can't get through.

CALLER: Uhm. . . well. . .

OPERATOR: Look, if this is a prank, you oughta be ashamed of yourself for holding up the show and spreading death and prolonging misery in countless other lives. Hello, hello, hello. . .

CALLER: I'm here.

OPERATOR: Somebody right now could be holding up a blue baby that has precious seconds to be resuscitated. You are sick, you need help. In this context you are tantamount to an abortionist. Look, you and your prank have pushed me over the edge. You know we have terrible working conditions: we don't get coffee breaks, and we take calls in a bunker four floors below downtown!

CALLER: Can I get in a word edgewise?

OPERATOR: Make it snappy.

CALLER: OK, here's the deal. My mother has stopped breathing. Please send an ambulance and paramedics.

OPERATOR: Oh my gosh, we'll send one right away, sir.

CALLER: Take your time. She stopped breathing six hours ago.

The Verdict

Each second of the interminable wait in the oncologist's office was eternity for Tess Cochran. She watched the clock, fidgeted with her cell phone, even skimmed *Oprah* magazine. Then, finally, the door at the end of the hall opened, projecting two silhouettes. In outline Dr. Frolich patted the tall, gaunt silhouette on the shoulder and looked commiseratingly.

The door shut and the man with whom Tess had shared life's best moments separated from the tall, gaunt shadow. All four feet ten inches of him emerged in the waiting room.

Harry looked at her forlornly, pronounced one word, "Positive."

Tess beamed from ear to ear and clutched him in a hug.

"Positive! That's great," she gushed. "Hallelujah! The power of positive thinking."

"Tess, no. You really are a dumb blond bimbo. In a medical context positive is not good, it's bad. I'm gonna be dead in six months."

"You don't get the picture, Harry," she squealed. "I'm gloating over all the tax advantages of you dying this year."

"I get the picture, Tess," said Harry. "The beneficiary of the tax breaks will be Phyllis, my wife."

Miracle

12/31/2010 – 11:59:31, Cedars-Sinai. A doctor gravely nods his head. The nurse tacitly understands the signal to remove the feeding tube and disconnect the cumbersome breathing apparatus. A daughter, father, and brother stand glumly at the bedside in the ICU.

ROCHELLE: Dad, it's OK to cry.

(They hug. After the nurse wrings out Rochelle's shoulder, father, daughter, and brother resume talking.)

DAD: You know one overriding factor—by some fluke Congress neglected to renew the estate tax this year. That means we wouldn't have to spend a cent for her real estate in Boca Raton or her 1918 inverted airmail stamp. Then there's been the gap in long-term care health insurance.

ROCHELLE: Wow! I can't believe you said that, Dad.

DAD: I'm sorry, Rochelle, you must think I'm some kind of greedy monster, thinking about money at a time like this. It's just something I needed to factor in. . .

BRYAN: (*smoldering*) It's not cruel or ruthless. It's reality. Fact is, we could have pulled the plug months ago. It's your fault I'm missing Lady Gaga at the Meadowlands this weekend. . .

ROCHELLE: For your information, Dr. Kervorkian, I have a heart. For months I brought Mom her favorite flowers, purple mums, and talked to her.

BRYAN: You were wasting your breath, Rochelle. The coma lasted seven months. . .

ROCHELLE: People have come out of comas after thirty years. There was this guy in Rumania. . .

BRYAN: Christ sake, you could have pulled the plug when Ruthie was here. We were all together for the holidays. Sam had flown in from Berlin. All of us could have attended the memorial. It would have been so convenient and. . . heartwarming.

ROCHELLE: Bryan, I know it's a long shot, I held out the hope Mom might still surprise us all. There was this guy in Rumania. . .

BRYAN: Dreams! Dreams! When are you going to face the facts: you'll never be Meryl Streep. You should have married Freddy Sturgeon when you had the chance.

DAD: Children, let's be civil and consider all the things you can get with the tax savings. Rochelle can get all the acting lessons she wants; you, Bryan, can live in France. Like the taxman says: the family that saves together, stays together. . .

(Father, son and daughter, chuckling conspiratorially, elbow nudge each other.)

ROCHELLE: Dad, to tell the truth, I've been struggling with the same thing. Arnie Ross's brother-in-law is an accountant and he was talking about it. I was afraid to say anything. I was worried you'd think I was cruel or heartless. With the tax savings, I *could* get that fox-grey 12-cyllinder Beamer I've had my eye on.

(The mother, Lazarus-like, rises on one spindly elbow, peers out, her gaze unfocused. There's a catch in Rochelle's throat, "Oh my god, Mom's alive." Brother and sister team up to put a pillow over mom's face and smother her. Then, before the task can be completed, Rochelle looks over and sees her father passed out cold on the hospital floor. He's gone straight to rigor mortis, his morning cup of Starbucks held straight up heavenward.)

Lewd

I never saw the new owner of the cottage after she moved in, but the lights were on at night across from me. She must have been in the bedroom mostly. One morning I glimpsed her in the yard and heard her wispy voice and the holler of a black man. OK, she had a black boyfriend. That was OK. Then I saw her leaving the place in a hurry and she threw a glance back at me down the walkway, her face pinched, and said *Is everything OK?* like maybe there was something that wasn't. I said *Everything is OK*. She said *That's good*, and added, *I need to get to my house.*

But her feet were taking her away from her house. It took another day or so for it to sink in that the guy in the cottage was not her boyfriend. People were coming and going. They didn't look at me when I said hello, or when they did look their gaze was shallow. Drugs, of course, but some of the

71

people looked too nice for druggies. Then it dawned. The cottage was being rented out as a bed-and-breakfast. From then on, I decided to say hello louder. Let them know somebody else was here; they were invading someone's home.

The newest B&B guest came down the walkway one night as I was leaving to pick up my clothes from the laundromat. The bells rang on the gate as the Swedish woman slipped inside. That afternoon I had felt like such a dork trying to talk to her as I avoided her eyes and my gaze kept falling on other parts of her body. I'd feel dorky all over again if I said 'Hello' in the night and it freaked her out. So I let her go inside without knowing that I was standing there, looking at her in the dark.

Then I went on my way. About halfway down the walk, a guy in a Clippers jersey came slouching along. He said to me, "You have a smoke?"

He kept on slouching all the way into the back reaches of the walkway and the darkness that separates my cottage from the bed and breakfast. I kept waiting for the dude to come back out into the moonlight. Maybe he was sitting in the lawn chair back there, wishing for a smoke. I was wary about leaving. He might jump a fence and try to break in, but the intruder seemed awful mellow for a burglar. He didn't come out, and he didn't come out, and I didn't want to face him, either:

I had to leave soon, or I would be locked out of the laundromat, and I'd have to pick up my clothes the next day. The way my week was shaping, this would mean wearing stinky clothes all week. I couldn't wait around anymore.

When I got back from the laundromat thirty minutes later, three black-and-whites were out front. I hollered to a lady cop just before she drove off, "He'll be spending the night with us," she said with a grin. "He did something lewd."

We were both grinning.

I know that wasn't how I was supposed to react, but my face was grinning, and the lady cop was doing it too.

When I walked back into the courtyard with my bag of laundry, I saw the big open front window in the B&B cottage. Easy to see what had happened. Poor horny sonofabitch got a full view of the Swedish woman. I feared a break-in and here he had followed her into the courtyard and got his rocks off while peeping through her window.

Next morning the new owner of the cottage was talking my ear off and saying the guy was going to come back. He was going to stalk the place and she wanted to spray him with mace. She carried mace. She wanted to cut off his balls. All this violent crap masking her fear that business would drop off. It took me to places I didn't want to go before coffee. The cottage court had become coarser now that strangers came in and out, and I had a neighbor who was never a neighbor, but I tried my best to be one and listen. Meanwhile, my morning espresso went cold and it was down hill from there.

Spooked

The Two-Year Itch

It was unavoidable. The Conversation had replayed so many stinking times Matt could recite it in his sleep:

–You're not *the* Matt Damon?

–I'm Matt Daemon with an 'e.'

–Are you an actor?

–Yes, I act, write, produce, direct, and do the valet parking thing on the side.

Now Matt elicited a chuckle from the secretary of the building management firm that had been hassling him on the phone about the rent. If he fled back home to Nebraska he could stiff them. After two years seeking the rainbow's end in Hollywood he was entering the dicey phase of the two-year itch—the critical time when hopefuls sink or swim.

Many, a good many, paddle on home with their dreams in a body bag.

Matt pocketed his phone. Cayetano, his supervisor, called him into his cubicle in the exhaust-scented bowels of a Sunset Boulevard hotel, "I told you before. No personal calls. We don't care about your rent or auditions or your girl trouble," Cayetano said. "You're fired."

Matt stood there and gawked at him.

"You heard me. You're fired! And turn in your red vest on your way out."

After getting canned by Cayetano, Matt shrugged, he checked in impulse to key the side of the Rolls Phantom, bit the cuticle of his forefinger. Above ground, Matt gazed on Sunset Boulevard where so many dreams had come true. The curtain was lowering on his dreams. Time to gather his belongings, reclaim his prized lens from the pawnshop (the camera had long since sold), and commence the long drive back to Nebraska.

He dreaded seeing the same old gang at the Dairy Queen. Anybody in Normal, Nebraska, with an ounce of ambition had high-tailed it. Joey the stoner, Tiffany the ex-cheerleader, Jose inherited the Chevy dealership from Daddy. They would all look at him as this pathetic loser. Only twenty-two months before they'd promised to come out and see his star on Hollywood Boulevard. Tiffany vowed to polish the brass edging around the pink mica star. Yeah, he'd get those pitying looks reserved for someone riddled by a flesh-eating disease.

Matt walked out to his Nissan Sentra and did the usual maneuver of opening the passenger lock first: the key didn't work on the driver's side. As he walked around the car with one crushed headlight, he spied the yellow steel wedge strait jacketing the front tire. He'd been booted. Crap! If he couldn't afford to get his car lock fixed, he sure couldn't afford to pay all his parking tickets and get his wheels back.

When he saw Cayetano leave the hotel garage, lunch box under his arm, Matt went back inside.

"Loan me a car, please," he begged to his friend Tony. "I just got booted, man."

Tony reluctantly gave Matt the keys to the Phantom. It belonged to an 18-year-old rapper from Jersey.

"Mr. Hip-Hop is on a binge in Vegas. Be careful. If Cayetano finds out. . ."

"He'll fire me,"Matt said.

"Whatever you do," Tony warned him, "anything happens to this car, this Stradivarius on wheels, it's"—he did a throat-slitting gesture with his hand.

Matt reached Cahuenga Boulevard and beelined for his small bungalow, still full of Linda. Her smell. Her jar of cold cream. Closed the gate and clicked the padlock. To keep out those damn cats and there'd been a burglary rumored by the neighbors—mostly single women and actor-director-screenwriter-valet parking-bartender types like himself. Matt spooned tuna fish out of the can. He wanted to call someone. Linda, no. Mom? Mom was always pleading to come home to Nebraska and find Jesus. He left the empty tuna can on the floor. That kind of slob thing a woman would housebreak: leaving his clothes on the floor and eating food out of the can.

Matt watched a little ESPN and dozed off on the couch. Then later, he didn't know how much later, he heard a scratching, a persistent scratching. Just one of those damn cats that roamed the courtyard—he chalked it up to feline intruders. But the sound continued, punctuated by a dry clicking sound, like pebbles on glass. He sat up from the couch. Outlined in the window, silvered by the neighbor's porchlight, stood a figure obscured in inky shadows. Despite all the darkness there was this live presence of that zapped him in the heart. Matt took one step forward and groggily called out:

"Hello."

The figure dipped from sight. Feet rustled in the grass. The hairs on Matt's neck bristled and tingled. It was unnerving to have a person on the other side of the glass. He went to the porch barefoot and looked at the gate. Locked tight. A smell of lilacs drifted in the air, and there was not a trace of anybody having been there.

A Slice of Heaven

In Lilac Zone, the ethereal residence of star-crossed actresses, you could bump into the platinum goddess, Jean Harlow, see Marilyn Monroe doing the New York Times crossword, always asking Jayne Mansfield for help with clues (Mansfield had a 149 IQ), and hear Lupe Velez, the Mexican Spitfire, gripe about being typecast as the Mexican Spitfire ("I am serious actress.") Then there was Lulu LaPeer; Clara Bow was the 'it' girl, and Lulu LaPeer the 'almost it' girl.

Lulu sat full lotus on a hot pink cloud and leafed through the latest *Variety*. As she read the assortment of predictable showbiz items, an exquisite boredom played around her classical features, then abruptly, her doe eyes popped out of her head and twirled like protons around a nucleus when she read that a new production of *Anna Karenina* was about to start shooting. Matt Damon was slated to play Vronsky, the count who refuses to get divorced, and propels Anna, his married lover, toward tragedy. The convulsive tidbit was enough to wake Lulu up from the Lilac Zone. The complex role of Anna, the role of a lifetime, combining mother, adulteress, and über sensitive soul, would have cemented Lulu's place in the 1920s pantheon and established her tragic acting chops. Alas, it had been denied her.

The celebrated likes of Marilyn Monroe wound up in Lilac Zone for all eternity. Just so long as their performances kept moving people, their celluloid incarnations flickering in the darkness, their heartbreak eyes and kissproof lips still seducing cinephiles, they would endure in flower-scented limbo. Not Lulu. A day after reading about Matt Damon and Anna Karenina in *Variety*, the last earthly shred of her acting career was eradicated: a nitrate copy of "Mommy Long Legs," a silent slapstick short, ignited and torched an abandoned movie theater in Kansas City.

Yawning luxuriantly, Lulu awoke in the heart of Hollywood, near Sunset and Vine, ready to pursue her dream of making a 'talkie' and to claim the title role of Anna Karenina. In the wee small hours she visited the cottage where she'd trysted with a mobster, Johnny "Panini Killer" Palma. Notorious for sautéing his victims' hands on a panini grill, Palma tried to bribe Lulu out of the running for Anna Karenina and pave the way for a new sweetheart.

"Over my dead body," Lulu shouted in the Brown Derby.

"That can be arranged," Johnny coolly replied.

She double-crossed Johnny, took his money, but didn't give up pursuit of the title role in *Anna Karenina*. Setting up a panini grill in the cottage kitchen proved unwieldy. Instead, Johnny's henchmen blew out the pilot flame in the oven, turned up the gas, and shoved Lulu's brunette head into the oven. Held her there till her body went limp. It looked like a suicide because she had been so broken up over Johnny picking up with a new dame—Dame May Whitty. In the end, Palma's girl lost out. The role went to icy, peerless Garbo and her onscreen romance with John Gilbert heated up the screen. . .

After landing in 21st century Hollywood and spying through the living-room window, Lulu was terrified when a voice inside said, "Hello." She sprang into the branches of a tall avocado tree, where she waited until morning. A yawning young man sauntered outside the cottage and got behind the wheel of the Rolls-Royce Phantom. "Must be well-to-do," she thought.

When the coast was clear, Lulu shimmied down the avocado tree. The gate was open, but the house was locked tight. She saw some letters in the mailbox and saw the addressee: Matt Damon. Lulu put it all together—the Rolls-Royce Phantom and Matt Damon! She was about the luckiest girl this side of lilac. She would emulate Garbo's method and woo the role by wooing her leading man.

Practically levitating, Lulu walked down Cahuenga.

Matt Daemon, with an 'e,' was cruising down Sunset in the borrowed Rolls-Royce Phantom, a plum-colored dream, en route to the Da Vinci Hotel.

Upon return from Vegas, the hip-hop king would find his thoroughbred wheels in their rightful place in the hotel parking garage. And nobody would be any the wiser.

The light turned green. Matt, the former valet parking jockey, pressed the accelerator, feeling the phenomenally powerful car respond to the lightest touch of his foot. Going against the red, a Plymouth Duster to Matt's right kept right on plowing through the intersection, and rammed into his side with a cacophonous, steel-wrenching crash. Matt's heart stopped.

Love, Sweet Love

The slow hiss of a punctured radiator replaced the gut-wrenching cacophony. Matt leapt out of the car and unleashed his fury on the driver of the Plymouth Duster, still holding a phone to her ear.

"You T-boned me," Matt bellowed.

"Everything is great, Pepe," the woman kept talking to the cell. "Gotta go. That's nothing, Pepe. Somebody's making a movie here. B'bye. That's what all that noise is."

"T-boned me while talking into a cell phone."

"Pepe will kill me," the woman squealed, lowering the phone from her ear. "My insurance goes up. Again."

Matt plunged into a vat of compost—well, it was something smellier and slimier than compost. He was a dead man and yearned to be back in Normal, Nebraska. Back hanging with Joey the stoner, and Tiffany the cheerless ex-cheerleader. Dude who owned the Phantom would kill Matt dead. He was dead, the lady in the Duster was dead; everybody dead. The eyes of a young thing, standing on the sidewalk, penetrated the vortex of doom: supernaturally bright, her jade eyes had the intensity of a leopard ready to pounce in a jungle.

The woman in the Duster reached down into her wallet and pulled out several bills. "Is that enough? Here's more," she pressed the bills into Matt's palm. "This never happened, OK?"

Sooner than Matt could count the pleasing denominations, the brunette with the supernatural eyes and the funny looking old-fashioned hat was all over him. Wiping him with a kleenex, solicitously scrutinizing him for scratches and wounds.

"Poor thing," the vintage chick bleated, "Are you all right?"

Matt was already late. He was sweating to get the Rolls back to the garage before the boss, Cayetano, came in. He'd already lost an hour cruising on Sunset and flirting with two blond twins in a convertible. He did a quick tabulation of his options: try to explain to police how he'd "borrowed" the Rolls Phantom or spend the day with the vintage chick. I think I'll go with the vintage chick, he decided. The money the lady had given him turned from rent into stardust. No matter. His confidence soared as he surveyed the damage: a nick on the front fender as the woman swerved to avoid the Phantom and wrapped her fender around a lightpole. The kind of ding easy to chalk up to a careless valet parker. Matt knew: as a valet parker he'd earned the moniker 'King of Ding.'

Now the Duster, still hissing, miraculously started up and limped away. Matt regretted not getting the lady's phone number—he might feel OK now, but something could still turn up and take him to a chiropractor.

"What's your name?" Matt asked the girl.

"Lulu. . ."

"I'm Matt. . ."

After they shook hands, he still kept looking at her, entranced.

"You can release your grip on my hand," Lulu reminded Matt.

"Oh, sorry," he looked down at his hand still in hers.

Then Matt offered Lulu the best thing he could offer, a spin in the Rolls Phantom. By force of habit, he jogged around to open the passenger side lock, the only one that worked in his own decrepit car. But being already next to Lulu, Matt did the gallant thing and opened the door of the Rolls for her.

"23 Skidoo," she squealed happily. Matt stared at her:

"You talk funny."

They drove to the beach. All along the way she exclaimed about the orange groves and open spaces had vanished, replaced by strip malls and pastel-colored apartments. So many changes. A couple kids were playing near the beach parking. Matt poked one in the shoulder: "Here, I'll give you five bucks if you watch my car. See that nobody touches it."

"Yes, sir!" the freckled boy said, bursting with pride.

"The ocean is still here," Lulu exclaimed when they reached the shore. "That's one thing that hasn't changed. I used to come out here with Mabel Normand, and nobody recognized her. We were just like anybody else. Nobody expected to see Mabel on the beach. Of course the name doesn't ring a bell with you. I guess I'm dating myself."

"You do seem mature," Matt said. "I mean, you look young but you've got a lot of experience. You're 22—25 years old max."

"Naturally," she said, bare feet kicking up the sand. "I was born in 1902."

Matt looked at her, narrowing his eyes. Then he let out a chuckle, "Aw you're messin' with me!"

"What is this, 'messin' with me'?"

Matt stared at her. Why couldn't she understand plain English?

"Messin' with me?" he spoke slowly, deliberately. "You know, like messing with somebody's head."

"Sorry, I don't understand," she shrugged.

"You know what," Matt said. "You not only talk funny. You listen funny."

Cinderella Night

The sun was a molten bowling ball ready for its rendezvous with the Pacific Ocean as Matt and Lulu strolled down the beach.

"Have you ever thought about acting?" Matt said. "I bet the camera loves you."

"You're the bees knees." Lulu fluttered her eyelids.

"It's funny. We've hardly talked about ourselves. That's usually the first thing people do in Los Angeles do."

"Often the only thing," Lulu said. "Back in my day. . ."

"Let's not talk about ourselves," Matt said, placing a finger to her lips. "Let's just be human beings for one magical night."

"What a charming idea!"

It fit perfectly with her coy ploy. As seductress, hell bent on the lead role in his upcoming remake of *Anna Karenina*, Lulu preferred not to talk to Matt Damon about himself. She knew it would be irresistible for a star like Mr. Damon, to have a vacation from himself.

Soon Matt held her hand and planted his lips on hers as reflected sun blazed gold in the windows of the beach houses.

After their walk on the beach, Matt and Lulu reached the "borrowed" Rolls.

"Thank you Jeeves," Matt said to the toothy, freckled kid who'd guarded it. Jeeves!? Just by hanging out with this girl, Matt thought he was starting to talk funny, too.

"Hey, where's my five dollars?" the kid sneered.

"I promised you five *bucks*." Matt got down on his hands and knees, "Come on, I'll give you your pony ride. All the bucks you want."

The kid made a sour expression. Matt got up, patted him on the back.

"Hey, I was just messing with you."

He pressed a ten-dollar bill to his palm. The kid grinned ear to ear.

"See that?" he said to Lulu. "I was messing with him."

"I haven't the foggiest idea what you mean, so stop trying," Lulu said. "Sometimes I think the only place where people remotely understand each other is in the movies.'

Inside the car, Lulu testily took out a cigarette from a sterling case. After an eon in the Lilac Zone, the corner of heaven reserved for ill-fated actresses, Lulu was about to give that Garbo, who'd snatched the role of Anna Karenina from her in 1926, a master class on how smoking was really done.

"No smoking," Matt barked.

"What are you mad about?"

"Get out of the car if you're going to smoke. That's a rule. And I'm not mad."

"But you're a smoker."

"How do you know?"

"I just know," Lulu said.

"Out. Out. Not in the car," he said steely.

"You're still cranky. I'm so famished I could eat two horses. It feels like a hundred years since I've eaten," Lulu said. "I'd like a swanky joint. If you haven't been out in as long as I've been in, you want something classy. Like the Cocoanut Grove."

"Your wish is my command," said Matt.

"It's on Wilshire. In that new hotel across from the Brown Derby."

"I'm not sure I know what you're talking about," Matt said.

They got to the site of the Ambassador Hotel, once home of the Cocoanut Grove, and gazed upon a field of dust. "This is it," Lulu said. "There're the bungalows where Scott bathed Zelda's feet in champagne."

"Scott and Zelda?" Matt asked.

"Some old acquaintances. They're gone, the hotel is gone." Lulu teared up, "Why must all beauty perish?"

"It's why things are beautiful. Like sunsets. Because they're around only a few seconds, then whoosh!" Matt's line cribbed from a high school play was intended to give comfort, but to judge from Lulu's watery mien, it didn't work. Take 2: "I figure it's like the garbage, honey," Matt spoke from the heart. "All the old beer cans and moldy pizza—you gotta take it out or it starts stinking up the place."

Matt's words had the effect of further opening Lulu's tear ducts. He knew what to do: take her to the bowling alley on Highland. Bowling could cheer anybody up. He splurged on valet parking: he had to keep up the charade of being a big shot. Matt barked to the valet parkers—members of the red-vest league to which he had belonged a very short time ago.

"I don't want so much as a speck of dust on this car. Not a speck. I know exactly what the odometer reads, right down to the last tenth of a mile."

Inside the dark rathskeller of the bowling alley, Matt and Lulu studied the menu on the wall. He ordered a beer and she, a club sandwich and a "Mary Pickford." The bartender had never heard of a Mary Pickford, Lulu settled for a margarita.

The order for the "Mary Pickford" brought Matt's suspicions to a head.

"I know we agreed not to talk about ourselves, but could I ask you something personal?"

"Of course." She eyed him over the rim of margarita.

"You remember a city that's vanished and use lots of weird expressions—"

Lulu gulped and tingled inside, fearing Matt had unmasked her immortal status.

A Boulevard Stroll

Matt's lips puckered around a consonant—a W to be exact. Lulu braced herself for the question, imploring him with her eyes to stop. At length, after he raised his voice a few giga-decibels over the thundrous bowling balls and the sizzling techno beat, she heard:

"Why were you in prison?"

Lulu gazed at Matt, dumbfounded, for an eternity, and then she let out an unbridled peal of laughter.

"Me? In jail!" she pointed to the crepe bodice of her flapper dress. "Why on earth would you ever think such a thing?"

"Your retro clothes."

"Retro?" she said and her eyes glazed.

"And your weird way of talking," Matt said. "I think you've done some serious time."

"Done time?" she mouthed. There was that glazed look again.

"Yeah," he said. "Or you were really born in 1902."

Lulu was silent for a long moment.

"Oh, I was pulling your leg about that. I'm really much younger."

Under further questioning, she lied to Matt that she had grown up around a great grandmother who'd given her the flapper dress and used lots of old-fashioned expressions, like bee's knees and 23 skidoo. Her innocent spontaneity, so prominent when she was fresh from Lilac Zone, the nook of heaven reserved for ill-fated actresses, now shriveled like a squash blossom at the first rays of sun. When she saw contraptions that automatically raked away the toppled bowling pins, she fought the impulse to burst out, "Twenty-three skidoo! I feel like I'm in the 23rd century." In Lulu's day a kid picked bowling pins up by hand.

Amid the grumble of bowling balls and crescendos of flying pins, Matt's seduction continued, the seducer not knowing he was the seduced. Matt cuddled Lulu's lithe body as he showed her how to step forward in the lane and swing the weighty ball upward, prelude to the ball's drop and release. She could feel his breath on the back of her neck. Her ruthless ambition to woo Matt and nab the role of Anna Karenina in his upcoming remake of *Anna Karenina* morphed into something more. Little did she know that this Matt Damon was Matt Daemon with an 'e,' but that's the kind of mistake you make when you're fresh out of Lilac Zone.

When they left the bowling alley, snuggling and giggling, they took a detour to the Boulevard. Their feet tread over the stars embedded in the glittery sidewalk. Greta Garbo's was highly buffed and polished. The brass fringe around the Pepto-Bismol colored star shined like a rill of fresh lava. Lulu paused to gaze upon it.

"Somebody must take good care of it," she said. "Not every star on the boulevard shines so brightly."

She stayed behind Matt a moment and discreetly spat on the star of Garbo, who had wrested Anna Karenina from her in the 20s.

Matt and Lulu advanced into the storybook land of Hollywood Boulevard. Spider Man was mugging for Swedish tourists. As Frankenstein and Wonder Woman stood around waiting for something to happen, Jesus of Hollywood, donning white burlap robes, was having his photo taken alongside tourists from Arkansas and a whip-toting dominatrix.

Matt paused among the clustered tourists and got out his phone. "Could you take a picture of us?" he asked Lulu, handing her the phone. "Just press the button."

Matt put his arm around Jesus' shoulder and Lulu commemorated the moment. Then Jesus of Hollywood offered to take a picture of them on the Boulevard. After they continued to stroll, Matt called home to Nebraska. "Just a sec," he said to Lulu, and to the phone: "Mom, it's Matt. I wanted to tell you I just found Jesus. This is for real. He's standing in front of the Chinese Theater, wearing a burlap dress."

Matt and Lulu resumed their walk and passed by a mustachioed man donning a bowler and twirling a cane.

"That isn't the *real* Chaplin," Lulu said. "He doesn't, ur. . ."

"What?" Matt said.

"Nothing," she said. "I was thinking out loud."

On their way back from the stroll, they stepped over a tarnished star. It hadn't been washed in years; it was dotted by black gobs of squashed chewing gum. There was the name in tarnished gold letters: Lulu LaPeer. It was all she could do to hold back the tears and not tell him that she had been the second most popular star for one whole week in 1925, right after Gloria Swanson.

In a subdued mood, Matt and Lulu got back from the boulevard stroll. The valet parker presented the "borrowed" Rolls, motor purring, keys inside. A yawning paparazzi snapped a few. Figured anybody who had a Rolls Phantom might be somebody, and the retro girl was cute.

In the plum-colored Rolls, Matt and Lulu cruised noiselessly into the night. Afterward, the photographer gawked at the shots. Matt and the car appeared, but the figure of Lulu had completely vanished. Not even the faintest shadow of a shadow appeared.

Dateline: Heaven

An alarm went off, a beeping red light in the office of Mr. Beardsley, manager of the whole celestial outfit.

"You see, they've noted an irregularity," Beardsley said to his intern. "It happens quite often in these transitional cases."

Jones raised a brow. Things were generally sedate in actress heaven, and Jones had looked forward to catching up on a lot of sleep apnea when Mr. Beardsley took his first vacation in eighty years. In Dahlia Zone, the lair of the Great Actresses, who were resigned to be here for as long as their performances were on view, on cable channels and at home theaters, nothing ever happened. Your Hepburns and your Bette Davises busied themselves with shuffleboard and karaoke night. Now Jones was learning heaven wasn't all a bed of dahlias; there were lilacs—the troubled, ill-fated divas.

"It could be a glitch in the paperwork," Beardsley went on. "Somebody didn't dot a T or cross their I's. Oops! I mean cross their T's and dot their I's. I really need that vacation!" Beardsley chuckled. "The provisional person is on parole. They have one foot in both worlds. Their old dreams and memories are still intact, and they are tethered to their earthly ambitions. It creates all kinds of snafus. Lulu LaPeer, for example, has fallen for the wrong Matt Damon. Because she lusts for a part in his next movie—has lusted for it from the day that Garbo snatched the role from her. And now, as a provisional from the Lilac Zone, she cannot be photographed, no image will appear—that's quite a pickle for a screen actress. The rub is: when Lulu is fully enfleshed on earth again, she will be a clean slate, free of the memory of ruthless ambition. To be Anna Karenina will be forgotten."

"And the love. . . ?"

Beardsley sighed and ignored the question. At length, he spoke:

"Tell me, Jones, do you like to travel?"

"Ye-es."

"Well, take a trip to earth and check up on Lulu for me."

After Matt and Lulu strolled down Hollywood Boulevard, Matt felt himself falling into the wishing-pool depths of those jade-green eyes. Lulu, Lulu, his heart sang. Matt decided to shoot the moon and took her to the place he knew best: the Da Vinci Hotel located discreetly off the Sunset Strip. Within minutes, he pulled up to the entry portico, and left the Rolls Phantom with the valet parker.

"Why it's the King of Ding," Tony said. Matt wanted to shush him like crazy, and with a jerk of his head alluded to his beautiful passenger, Lulu, hoping that Tony would take a hint and pipe down. Instead of piping down, Tony strolled slowly around the full perimeter of the Phantom, applying his practiced gaze to the car body and the metallic plum paint.

"The King of Ding does it again," Tony said. "Did you piss off somebody tonight, huh? The whole passenger side has been keyed. Cayetano will kill you."

Tony gracefully opened the door for Lulu. He came back and opened for Matt who whisper-shouted to Tony, "Shut up. She thinks I'm a big shot." A few bills exchanged hands and Brooklyn-born Tony still didn't shut up. "She's a real hottie," he said in what passed for a low tone of voice in him. "That Rolls must be a girl magnet."

Matt glanced at Lulu. She seemed to be occupied under her funny bell-shaped hat, drinking in the Da Vinci Hotel and its gardens. Matt prayed that the fountain had drowned out Tony's words.

Inside the hotel Matt's buddy, the bellhop, uttered a reverential "Good evening, Mr. Daemon." That bellhop must have been afflicted by Cupid, too, for he pressed a key into Matt's hand, and after giving a wink, said, "Follow me."

Moments later, Matt and Lulu entered a penthouse suite. The whole city, its pulsating matrixes of light, kneeled before them.

"It's gorgeous," said Lulu, surveying the amazing view.

"We're up so high we oughta have oxygen masks," Matt said.

Their lips met. Matt breathed in her smell of earth and lilac, and the silk sheets beckoned. Lulu tilted her head back so he could kiss her neck. A magnetic force drew them toward the bed in a tango-hold, and together they fell to the silky softness of the sheets, their limbs entwined. . .

Cinderella Morning

She awoke first, leaving Matt sprawled under silk sheets on a bed big enough to hold a croquet tournament. Lulu closed her eyes and tingled with voluptuous memory from the last night.

Lulu gazed at herself in the mirror, the funny bell-shaped hat perched on her head. Gazing out the picture window of the DaVinci Hotel: her eyes lighted on a billboard that loomed outside. It blazed publicity for a new flick starring the real Matt Damon. The five story cap-toothed kisser in the sky in no way resembled her Matt, but that typified Hollywood. In real life, Valentino didn't look a bit like his smoldering screen persona, Lulu recalled, he had droopy shoulders, a weak chin, and wore a hairpiece. He was the guy you'd ask to take the luggage upstairs.

Gingerly Lulu stepped over to Matt's pants, heaped on the floor, gingerly she went through his pockets, gingerly she removed the wallet. She scrutinized the California Driver's License. Damon was the actor, Daemon with an 'e' was the guy under the sheets—her eyes shifted from billboard to bed to license to billboard. Oops! With a knuckle-gnawing gesture, Lulu realized she had bedded the wrong Matt Damon in her pursuit of the Anna role in the remake of *Anna Karenina*, with Damon starring as Count Vronsky. This Matt was pretty low-rent, after all; had taken her to a bowling alley, for god's sake, instead of to the Brown Derby. How unromantic. And come to think of it, not a soul had asked for his autograph.

Matt roused and yawned tentatively. A dagger of panic pierced Lulu. To be caught with his wallet open in her hands didn't look good. In a blink, she slipped the wallet into the denim pants on the floor. A terrible scene awaited Lulu, a scene the long-ago silent movie princess dreaded playing. "I have to be going now," she would mumble. "Where?" "Off to auditions, to do the things actresses do." Then she'd be snared into an admission that she had used him as a stepping stone to the lead in the *Anna Karenina* remake.

After a brief encore of deep sleep, Matt moaned and slowly shook awake. His arm reached out for Lulu, and found nothing. His eyes opened wide, and he sat up from the silky tangle of sheets and looked out. There, Lulu stood wearing only a hat, and twenty floors below them, the kneeling city waited with the hum and promise of a new day.

"Awful, it's uh. . . I don't know how to say this, Lulu." Matt stuttered at the edge of a precipice. "I'm not who you think I am. I'm not a rich dude. That's not my Rolls-Royce that we rode in. I'm not a trust-fund baby. I'm a fired valet parker who came out here from Normal, Nebraska with big dreams. It was all a dream."

Lulu came over. She looked deep into his hazel eyes. Then she sat on the edge of the bed and embraced him, saying, "Without dreams we're dead." Her lips pressed hungrily against his. "Matt, I have my own confession to make," she softly spoke between long kisses. "I was really born in 1902." Then, just as he was processing what she'd said. . . poof! Lulu vanished. Jones from Lilac Zone had taken her back to where she belonged. One moment Matt was feeling flesh and beholding her jade-green eyes, an instant later, air. All around Matt looked—in the cavernous closets, under the immense bed: Lulu, Lulu, Lulu. Nothing—only a fragrant hint of lilac remained.

A wound opened in him. Disheveled, and full of love and ache, Matt stood in his skivvies in the enormous suite. Somebody pounded on the door, angry and impatient. The door flew open. In scowled Cayetano:

"I've been looking for your ass, Daemon," he said, temples throbbing. Matt braced. Cayetano went on, "I was driving in to work and saw Tony on Sunset Boulevard in the Rolls Phantom with two hookers. The nerve of that guy! And he tried to blame on you. Well, he's fired and you're hired."

Matt, flabbergasted, took it in stride. He knew to follow the actor's credo: always say yes. "Your vest is in the locker room," said Cayetano. Matt was already padding down the spongy hallway carpeting to the elevator, on his way to the parking garage, when he got a text message: Joey the stoner and Tiffany the ex-cheerleader were coming out on a road trip from Normal, Nebraska. Wow. That was Los Angeles: just when you thought everything was over, and it was time to head back to Normal, at the snap of a finger things started clicking all over again. What a beautiful world.

Heil Sig

Freud in New York the latest Otis Quigley Keefauver novel (Norton 897 pages) explores one of history's intriguing what-ifs: what if Sigmund Freud had sized up Hitler's threat sooner and immigrated to New York instead of London? This rambling but ambitious mish-mash of naiveté and fantasy was inspired by the amazing but true New York link in the Freud family.

In real life, Freud's nephew Edward Bernays was a brilliant adman who "sold" World War I to the American Public and used Freud's theories to break the taboo on females smoking in public. In 1930 he staged a march down Fifth Avenue and had debutantes defy convention and publicly puff "freedom torches," shamelessly exploiting the Freudian symbolism of the female mouth and phallic cigarette, overnight doubling the cigarette market for his client, the American Tobacco Company. In the novel, Eddie, who comes across as likeable but Machiavellian shlub, twists Uncle Sigmund's arm to come to New York, "We'll make a great team."

Sigmund's arm falls off, thus revealing that the great psychoanalyst's health is much worse than his doctors have led him to believe. His daughter Anna is especially relieved her father will be going to safer shores, even if it means missing the Berlin Olympics. (He was particularly keen about the javelin throw.) The hard-headed Freud has gruffly dismissed urgings that he leave Germany since 1932 and seems oblivious to the exodus around him, though his letters from the period routinely offer comments such as, "I saw a Mayflower truck in front of the Schoenbergs' today."

Once in New York, Freud stops long enough, to interrupt his new theory on the origins of coasters related to mankind's narcissistic self-hate, to accept an honorary doctorate at Columbia University. Freud gives graduating students this prescient and disturbing view from Europe, "There are indeed storm clouds brewing over Europe, but there is only a 5% chance of rain. . . They have burned books, before long they will be burning people," Freud predicts, shocking his isolationist audience—another of the historical inaccuracies that Quigley Keefauver revels in and expects the reader to be grateful for when it pays off in this novel's alternate universe.

Freud's health (during the period covered in the novel he had advanced oral cancer that had started in his mouth in the 1920's) was declining. The Bernays household which was well off but by no means wildly affluent were stretching the budget and sanity between medical expenses, the exorbitant bill for cigars from Alfred Dunhill, and Uncle Sigmund's beloved bratwurst smuggled weekly by Moldavian refugees who in turn had to be smuggled back home on weekends.

"It's costing and arm and a leg to keep you here," the nephew fumes. "Because of you we've defaulted on a second mortgage in the Catskills. Look, Uncle Sig, I'm the only guy who's ever really cashed in on the psychoanalysis thing."

"You and the cartoonists who use the couch," retorts an enraged Freud, who is enraged for many of the novel's 800 pages. "If I had a pfennig for every time one of those imbecilic cartoons appears. . ."

Eddie suggests that his uncle appeal to a mass audience. "Radio's the thing. I'm sure there's a place for you between 'The Shadow' and 'Fibber McGee and Molly.'

So Sigmund puts on his Homburg and goes to Radio City Music Hall. There his skin thrills at the sight of the synchronized dancers, and he becomes infatuated by a Rockette. A December-January romance ensues between Rhonda and Freud. He writes his dentist, Joseph Weinmann, "She is sufficiently comely to corroborate the primacy of lust as chief among emotions driving humans, and I think it's time to schedule a teeth cleaning." Freud follows Rhonda to Hollywood and becomes an avid jitterbugger, not great, but pretty good for a guy in the throes of stage 4. And he sees this American dance craze as a backlash to Victorian repression. When Rhonda is doing a K Flip and grabs the arm that was wired on by the Museum of Natural History, it gets yanked off and the crowd, horrified by the sight of the torn limb, stampedes out of Florentine Gardens.

Rhonda is presumed trampled to death. The only remnant left by which Sig can remember her is a mock turtleneck sweater. Freud is despondent because he cannot figure out what the turtle is mocking.

The second half of Otis Quigley Keefauver's ambitious new Freud-inspired fiction begins promisingly enough. After defeating Great Britain, Germany annexes it to the Reich.

Drunk on power, Hitler decides to have a plebiscite. At first no one knows what a plebiscite is, and they have everything fumigated. After the votes are counted, Hitler is ousted, peace breaks out and world war is averted, along with the atomic age. In one clever moment, Quigley Keefauver, spoofs Hannah Arendt's famous remark about the Nuremberg Trials—"the banality of evil"—and in this novel's boring but peaceful alternate universe Arendt has only the Andrews Sisters to decry as "the banality of banality."

Meanwhile, after the sudden fall of the Reich in 1937, Freud grows increasingly resentful of his dentist and daughter Anna who had urged him to leave Germany, causing him to miss the Berlin Olympics. He even starts to suspect his arch-enemy, Karl Gustav Jung, had a hand in getting rid of him, "to have the psychoanalytical crown of Europe all to himself."

The second half of *Freud in New York* has the distinguished émigré now working as night man at a newsstand. It's a win-win, because the experimental radiation treatments, started in Columbian Presbyterian Medical Center in return for his Honorary PhD speech were giving him a new lease on life, and his jaw makes an excellent reading lamp. During night shift at the magazine stand he actually gets around to reading *Moll Flanders*.

Sigmund still grieves for the loss of his great love, Rhonda, the showgirl trampled in the ballroom stampede, and has renounced intellectual life. In a letter to his dentist the father of psychoanalysis lashes out, "Because of alarmists like you and Anna, I have been made a laughing stock. If I live 1000 years, I shall never live down my gloomy comments about Europe made at Columbia University."

Meanwhile, the tide of unusual events causes Hitler to shave his moustache and legally change his name to Emmet Hitler. After a rough time in Paris, selling dirty postcards that smudged his customers' fingers, the clean-shaven former German strongman immigrates to Hollywood to pursue a childhood dream of joining a barbershop quartet. Here he buys a movie-star rag. A bearded, white-haired man who tends the magazine stand gives the customer change. The customer's hand flinches and pennies and nickels spill over the counter.

"I'm sorry," says the cashier.

"My fault," says Hitler.

"Classic transference of guilt. A lot of things were your fault, Mister, but not what just happened."

"Didn't you used to be someone," Hitler says.

"I was indeed," replies Freud. "And so were you."

Freud and Hitler shake hands and share a reflective moment, before Freud runs the former dictator off with a flyswatter after deeming the former Fuhrer has spent too much time ogling in the girlie magazine section.

The Hat

I got all the complements. It wasn't as if I fished for them. From the moment we teamed up, the complements started flowing. For some, I evoked 1940s panache; a cop said I made us look like a Miami drug dealer. A gap-toothed man who panhandles the traffic islands on La Cienega was reminded of his dad, "Had one just like that. Real stylish."

The only flak Mr. Miller ever got for me was that I, Panama extraordinaire, woven in Ecuador, lacked an intriguing story. Mr. Miller bought me from Nordstrom's. Plain and simple. The bulk of what he possesses: the pieces in his art collection, his Cuban cigars, his Italian loafers: each has a story. The cigars were from a yard sale, the loafers from Uncle Yeram the shoe repairman, the paintings—each and every one has a story from the bald eagle acquired at a swap meet in Chicago to the Matthew Heller bought with embezzled investor funds.

Friends would ask, "Where did you get that hat?"

"I bought it at Nordstrom's," Mr. Miller would reply sheepishly.

"That's not very interesting."

As a new hat I had no story to speak of, that is, until Memorial Day. Then everything changed. Returning with the groceries on Fountain, Mr. Miller made the mistake of doing too much at once: on top of taking the groceries in, a task that required both hands, he wanted to get me out of the suffocatingly hot car. To ready himself for the walk ahead, he stuck me—the Panama—atop the scraggly sweat-stained cap he was already wearing. Both hands were strained by the weight of groceries. And he was fuming because his daughter not only mocked the way he looked ("Wearing two hats looks funny," she said, squinting down her nose), she wouldn't accept one of the grocery bags: insubordination.

At Cahuenga they turned the corner, where a decent wind was blowing. And I sailed right off Mr. Miller's head. Because of the cap he was wearing, Mr. Miller didn't feel a thing. As the wind kept blowing I rolled like a quarter on the edge of my brim as cars speeded over me. Miraculously, I veered into the gutter came to rest at the feet of a bottle collector cooling his heels on the curb. The bottle collector took an immediate shine to me, put me on his head and resumed pushing his cart of bottles down the street.

A few minutes later, when Mr. Miller reached his house and put down the grocery bags, his hands felt above the cranial equator and he gasped, "My hat!"

A frantic sprint followed. Up and down the street he searched, behind fences and in parking lots. Secretly he was miffed at his daughter for not noticing when I flew the coop. Being close to Mr. Miller's thoughts, as his sombrero of choice, enabled me to accurately deduce his thoughts as he searched for me in vain, "If a nuclear bomb is ever launched

104

by accident, you can bet a child will have been in the room when it happened."

He doggedly crossed Fountain and walked as far as Funk Bros. and confirmed that I, his wide-brimmed eminence, had indeed vanished. It was devastating. Such good care he had lavished on me—not even a single bead of head perspiration had ever penetrated my ribbed silken band. Poof! Gone without a trace. Traumatized to the marrow, he gave up the façade of zen master, and phoned his therapist:

"When can I get an appointment," he said. "I'm devastated."

"Next Monday."

"Doctor, that's a long time. Doctor, please. . ."

"I'm not the doctor. This is the answering service."

"Listen, I'm going through the grieving process. I need help. . ."

"You know," said the operator, "sometimes you just have to let it go."

He hung up with a desultory gaze. His daughter observed:

"Dad, you look sad."

"I *am* sad."

"It's only a hat," she said.

"Dads need to pout sometimes. It's good to pout. Then you can look back and say I overreacted, that was so silly of me. It was only a hat. It would be nice if we could pout together. I've put up with plenty of your pouting. Now put up with some of mine."

After a while Mr. Miller grabbed a marker and he made a poster, *HAT LOST, on the corner of Cahuenga and Fountain, 2 p.m. Memorial Day. $$$ REWARD*

His daughter stared at him slowly forming the letters, compressed her lips, and said:

"You have to let it go."

Usually it's the grown-ups offering bromides that that children cannot apply, while the wound is too fresh. He wasn't ready for his daughter's breathtaking zen wisdom, I can tell you that. At this point Mr. Miller let out a primal scream to make the china plates tremble, to make the twigs shiver, to make a stranger look up and see a rakish Panama hat resting atop the hedge near the corner of La Mirada and Fountain, where I was stranded after the bottle collector discovered I was too small for his head.

"My what a fine looking hat," the dapper stranger thought.

On the outside Mr. Miller did his best to forget me and move on. After all, I was only a hat. Late at night, though, under the forlorn light of streetlamps, Mr. Miller toured Hollywood and taped posters, *HAT LOST, on the corner of Cahuenga and Fountain, 2 p.m. Memorial Day. $$$ REWARD.* His childishly drawn poster shared telephone poles with fliers for yard sales and missing pets. He would gaze into the eyes of lost Chihuahuas and Yorkie Terriers and Siamese cats, and wonder what people saw in them. Now a hat was something you could wear, it could keep your thoughts company, it gave one pizzaz, and you didn't have to feed it.

It strains credulity to describe as staggering the loss of something trivial as a hat. Yet to have lost so fine a hat, bought for good money and whose whereabouts remained unknown, was deeply troubling. But Mr. Miller seemed gradually to be getting over my loss as evidenced by a light-hearted trip to the hat store. Bowlers and Stetsons, straw and felt, wide-brimmed Panama's and snap-brim porkpies, jaunty berets and rakish Borsalinos—a dozen of them he tried on, each debuting a new personality. Yet none would quite do; there wasn't that chemistry he and I had.

Stooped by an irrevocable sense of loss, he left the shop.

The days went by. The missing hat posters fell from the telephone poles and blew in the wind, Hollywood sagebrush. In his daydreams a greedy scoundrel phoned Mr. Miller and demanded ransom for my return. But that's all it was—a fantasy. Moments after my loss, when Mr. Miller was plunged in dizzying despair, his daughter's precocious words had been a slap in face. They now came back to mollify him. *Your hat had a mission on earth, to teach you the impermanence of things, the transitoriness of life.*

"I'm getting over this thing," he told himself. "Why I haven't thought of my missing Panama for more than thirty seconds now."

It was almost a week since I had blown away, succumbed to the wicked wind of Cahuenga, which makes it the Bermuda Triangle of lost hats. Sunday was the Farmers' Market on Ivar. Mr. Miller and little Miss Miller strolled up the thoroughfare till the stands started dotting the side of the street shut to traffic.

Mr. Miller fondled some tomatoes and eyed a purple cabbage. Peering above a mountain of Valencia oranges, he saw something that made his heart quicken, his pulse race. Both mortified and elated—he spied me. His missing Panama hat! Amid the flowing locks of sunlit hair, the tattooed necks, perforated ear lobes, and the hoi polloi of baseball caps, he saw me and swooned. Propped on the globe-shaped head of a man in overalls leaning against a table of potatoes, chewing on a toothpick, the hat was the exact same dark ivory tone acquired by the smiles of a four-pack-a-day smoker and its brim described an elegant orbit around the woven crown. Mr. Miller was about to poke the farmer in the ribs and tonguelash him for hat thievery when he discerned on the hat's silver-tan band an archipelago of sweat stains. It wasn't me, or if it was me, he couldn't bear to see me blemished. He let out a whimpered cri de coeur.

Already another market patron with his missing Panama perched atop had caught the tail of Mr. Miller's eye. This hat wearer was inconspicuous, but for a bass fiddle he hauled on his back. You would think the easiest thing in the world would be trailing a man who hauls a bass fiddle on his back, but you'd be wrong in the Hollywood Farmers' Market. Among the warren of market stalls hawking herbs and tie-dyed shirts and falafels and the mob of Sunday people, the stocky man with the bass fiddle wove in and out of sight like a silver needle threading its way through sackcloth. The man with the bass was glimpsed and lost half a dozen times.

Mr. Miller and his daughter speeded up their steps through the mazy market and trailed the man. They were nearly onto the broad expanse of Vine when a loud "excuse me," had the effect of turning around the bass player, who was wearing his lost Panama.

"Where did you get that hat?" Mr. Miller said, short of breath.

"At the Nordstrom outlet in Pasadena."

"If it's not an indiscretion," Mr. Miller asked, "how much did you pay?"

The bass player replied with a figure a fraction of what Mr. Miller had paid in Nordstrom at the Grove. "Thank you," he said weakly. The bass player fell back into step, leaving Mr. Miller and his daughter alone.

"What's the matter?" his daughter asked.

"Nothing," Mr. Miller replied. It was the nothing children utter when they are at play building a small thermonuclear device. Ask "What are you doing?" and they reply, "Oh nothing." It shamed him to reveal that on top of the hat obsession he was now sore over a few lousy shekels discount somebody had gotten by shopping Nordstrom's outlet.

"Dad, where are you taking me," the young Miss Miller squealed when her dad grabbed her hand.

To the Gold Line they went, sucked down the throat of the metro entrance, bound for Pasadena and the Nordstrom outlet. They walked in the whirring train and held onto the rails as it swayed and sped in the darkness. Mr. Miller spied me again atop the head of a blurry face. I was flooded by joy: my rescuer had arrived. My sojourn on the dapper man's head had been no bed of roses. More than once I regretted not having been claimed under the tires of an 18-wheeler. Now Mr. Miller would redeem me, his beloved Panama, from the man with furtive eyes and the sweet-peaches aroma of a veteran lush.

"That's my hat," Mr. Miller spoke.

The man looked over with gummy eyes.

"I tell you, it's my hat," Mr. Miller sputtered. A gob of spit ejected from his lips and arced to the man's vest. He expressed apologies to the man in a vest matching pants fashioned of the same polyester, immaculately laundered and fastidiously buttoned. Likewise, his cheap necktie was perfectly knotted.

"Oh, I'm sorry to tell you," said Mr. Miller. "But it's still my hat."

His daughter looked on ashamed, just as two police came into the metro car.

"I got it as a present on Father's Day," said the man, indignantly.

Words escaped Mr. Miller. He looked like he was going to say something. Then he took his daughter's hand with suppressed violence and walked toward another car. My heart sank as their figures grew smaller and smaller in the rocketing metro car. Mr. Miller now sat at the end of the car and stared side to side, as if being stalked by his own cowardly avoidance.

Then Mr. Miller suddenly stirred. He stood and started walking towards me and to face the man who had me prisoner on his head. Closer and closer he came, trailed by his daughter. He'd remembered my one distinguishing trait: on the unblemished hatband a brownish droplet of his daughter's cola had left a barely perceptible watermark. At the time, Mr. Miller had been caring for me so well that the fizzy geyser of cola had provoked a spasm of anguish, and he snatched me off his head and subjected me to merciless inspection.

He reached my new owner, just as he prepared to get off the train. Mr. Miller tapped him on the shoulder.

"That's my hat. I know it's mine," his voice unwavering. The man laughed, showing teeth in need of cleaning.

"How can you tell?"

"The unblemished sweat band has one mark on the side from when my daughter's cola fizzed all over."

The blear-eyed man lifted me from his oily head and stared inside the crown.

"Oh, take it! Take it! It's yours," the man burst out, and pressed me into Mr. Miller's hands too fast for him to grab hold of. Before slipping out the open door onto the metro platform and losing himself in the gorgeous Sunday afternoon, the dissolute man fixed a baleful look on Mr. Miller that banished any trace of triumph in the recovery of his hat.

The metro doors hissed back together and pneumatically sealed; the train lumbered out of the station, bound for Pasadena. Mr. Miller stared down at me, the Panama hat on the floor. He reached down, picked me up, dusted me off and put me back onto his head. I was home again, home at last. Free from the demons that drove the dapper, dissolute man.

The man didn't even put up a fight! Mr. Miller thought. The man could have at least stuck to the flimsy excuse I was a Father's Day gift. But no: in his weakness the man had surrendered me without so much as a cross word.

In one violent motion Mr. Miller thrust me to floor of the train and trampled me. When I was flattened to a dead pancake, he sat back down by the train window and wept bitterly.

"Daddy," his little daughter asked in her little voice, "are you sad?"

Riot on the Southwest Chief

Raveendran Patel looked forlornly at the Kansas plains emerging from the dawn mists at daybreak, behind the panoramic glass of the observation car. There across the upholstered seat for two lay the sleeping woman who had turned down his desperate midnight plea to buy a few almonds from her. The greedy woman had said, "No," and went back to her romance novel. Her nose was the only thing showing from under a funny canvas hat that would have looked quite at home on a beekeeper.

After his failed attempt to acquire almonds, Raveendran consoled himself that he hadn't been turned down, rather the woman had denied his call to join with the universal source of supply. This take on events certainly didn't change matters, and Raveendran was still quite hungry.

He craved an apple, an orange, something natural as it had been created and packaged by Mother Nature. Something crisp and fleshy that he could sink his teeth into. Nothing else would do.

His cousin in Chicago had given him a fine send-off at a buffet on Devon Avenue, which had deprived him of the opportunity to buy and bring fruit aboard the train. While at the buffet he had wasted the chance to go to the salad bar and had chicken tikka masala, instead, and much garlic naan bathed in spicy tomato dipping sauce. He had severely neglected satyagraha, the vow to adhere to a diet of fruits, nuts and vegetables when in America.

At Union Station Raveendran had promptly boarded the Southwest Chief and then, filled by an urge to buy an apple or orange, retraced his steps and asked the woman who had scanned his ticket on the platform if he had time to go upstairs.

"The only thing I can tell you is this train leaves at 3:15," she said gruffly.

Raveendran Patel sulked back aboard the train: there had been plenty of time to run up to the store and stock up. Regret piled upon regret. The polished apples and oranges had seemed costly when he first spied them, walking to the train gate; but seeing the prices in the train's snack bar, not to mention the fact that they had never heard of an apple, revealed his mistake. His regret for not buying those apples and oranges back in Chicago grew deeper and deeper as they headed westward and he repeatedly went window shopping in the snack bar, in the futile hope that the prices would lower or that a navel orange would magically appear. Creation had always provided. Besides, what else was there to do? People could be engaged in conversation, but many of the Americans made faces before his pronunciation and said

"What!" And his name also caused them a great deal of trouble.

Raveendran Patel gazed bewildered for the umpteenth time at the same items for sale in the snack bar. His faith—faith that all his needs would be met—was severely tested. The stainless steel shelves offered a uniformly revolting selection of donut holes, Danish pastries sleeved in plastic, pizza pies, Angus beef hamburgers, hotdogs and sodas laced with sugar.

"Sir, what would you like?" the cashier asked.

"Nothing," he said. "I'm just looking."

While Mr. Patel gazed at the disheartening shelves, the cashier was talking to a customer about a passenger who had jumped off the train outside of Mendota, Illinois. "He tore open the door and threw his bags out. He wanted to get off the train, but we had to bring him aboard. We just can't leave somebody in the middle of nowhere," said the cashier. "There he was standing in a gulley in the middle of nowhere. He is 5150."

Another customer said, "Was he the guy in the red shirt?"

"He was wearing a red shirt that said: Keep calm and carry on," said the snack bar cashier. "5150. Certifiable."

Raveendran opted for a cup of coffee. It was the least impure thing on the menu and it would hold him over for a 25-minute Kansas City stop when Raveendran plotted making a break for it and finding a convenience store nearby. Meanwhile, at Fort Madison, Iowa after crossing the Mississippi, the doors opened and two policemen came aboard to escort the man in the red shirt off the train. He walked docilely onto the dry deserted platform. But just before the door closed and the train resumed its forward movement, he shouted, "A curse on this train for the way you treat smokers. There will be damnation and much gnashing of teeth before the City of Angels."

At Kansas City, where Ravendreen was sure they had heard of an apple or banana, a smoking break was scheduled. A whole 25 minutes. Long enough for Raveendran to make a mad rush, beyond the train station, in hopes there would be a store nearby where he could find an apple.

The porters posted on the platform outside the silver train cars made it sound like the train was due to leave any second now and leave Raveendran behind the in the dust. This set him on edge as he skirted around clumps of people with slender white cylinders in their mouths, breathing smoke in and out. If this was India they would have had a space aboard to the train to indulge their vile habit. But this wasn't India. Raveendran felt like such a criminal escaping the circumscribed world of the train and he scurried past the smokers and bounded up a steep flight up steps, passing a steady stream of sweaty passengers coming out of the waiting room, toting their bags on rollers. The causeway from the top of the stairs to the waiting room was unbearably long. Each new step away from the train weighed more on his conscience.

Hurry! Hurry! The train's going to leave without you. . .

At last, as Raveendran reached the waiting room, trimmed in honey oak wainscoting dating from the time of William Howard Taft's presidency—all the foot traffic pointed in the opposite direction, and yonder in the glassed-in waiting room, he saw the black flanks of vending machines for coke and candies. Somehow he didn't have the heart to actually look inside and see what rubbish they had on sale: certainly no apple or orange. He felt claustrophobia. His resolve to keep going outside and onto the streets of Kansas City suddenly eroded, almost as if the controls over his mind and body were in the hands of another. He could hear the train clanking away, and there would be nothing left by the time he reached the platform—only the dank smell of cigarette smoke, a few vanishing veils that hovered in the stagnant air. Seized by a panic of being stranded in Kansas City, he bounded back down the steep cement flight of stairs, still pursued by insatiable longing for something fresh and crisp.

Even the Dunkin Donuts glimpsed before boarding in Chicago filled him with longing—even though succumbing to the deep-fried realm would constitute the most flagrant flouting of satyagraha.

Into that known, refrigerated realm Raveendran returned, dogged by a sense of failure and entrapment. His ears were met by fellow passengers talking:

"We're an hour behind and we don't have wi-fi."

"I can't believe they don't have wi-fi. We're trapped on a train for three days and you think there'd be wi-fi."

"What I wouldn't do for a stalk of celery," a bright-eyed woman said. "My sister is dying for a peanut butter and jelly sandwich."

"My soul cries out for something simple," said Raveendran in his melodic accent.

Whaaaat? rasped the speakers, their faces screwed up.

He repeated himself again, slowly, and elicited still silent incomprehension. Raveendran gave up and capitulated to silence.

With a deep sigh he sat back down in his seat. By watching another passenger he learned the clever trick of pulling the lever and making the faux leather seat recline. Soon enough, due to the soothing darkness and fatigue, he imagined swaying in the gentle darkness and hearing the distorted clang of trestle bells swinging. Raveendran's eyes blinked open and his gaze was met by the same eerie yellow incandescence of the parking garage to the side of the tracks in Kansas City. The Southwest Chief had not progressed one inch westward.

Now he spotted smokers still scattered on the cement platform.

"Sir," he said to the porter. "Can I run up to the vending machines. Just five minutes."

Raveendran was resigned to the possibility of salted peanuts—at least a product of nature, even if the salt was man's doing. The porter shook his head glumly, dewlaps gathering above his stiff collar. He blocked the open door. In the time the porter and another passenger were talking, Raveedran could have run to and from the vending machines. Twice.

"Did you see the guy in the red shirt who got escorted off the train?" the porter said.

"The crazy man?"

"This wasn't the guy in the red shirt," said the porter. "This was another one who was smoking in the bathroom."

"No regard for others," the passenger spoke. "And the scout troop, none of those boys had a choice if they wanted to breathe that smoke."

The porter said smugly, "He will be banned for life from Amtrak."

I wish I had a banana peel and I'd leave it on the platform for one of these bleeding porters to slip on, Raveendran thought. He was a bit taken aback by his own growing belligerence. Finally, the train clattered into movement, and Raveendran fell into the most delicious drowsiness.

A muffled announcement came over the loudspeaker, "This is Garden City, Kansas. If this is your stop, get off here. This will be a brief stop. This will not be a smoking stop."

The tribe of smokers on board inwardly groaned. Soon afterward came the volley of words, "Can I sid down here?" The man with bulging tattooed biceps sat down as Raveendran stared out the observation-car curved glass at a new day dawning over the cornfields. The Southwest Chief clanked into forward movement again and Raveendran's mouth watered as the deserted train station fell away from view and revealed an Arby's and McDonald's. This was the American landscape working on him, slowly but surely wearing away his resistance to things thoroughly unappetizing and contrary to his ravenous desire for an apple or orange.

"I'm going to Bakersfield to see my sons," said the man. "They can have Bakersfield. The traffic, the noise, everything overpriced. Give me Garden City. California is madness; I wouldn't trade it for Kansas." He took off his baseball cap and scratched his dark wavy hair. "Bakersfield is getting as bad as Los Angeles. You couldn't pay me to go back to L.A. You can keep it. I wouldn't go there for all the rice in China. My doctor says, I go on a plane, 'you'll come back in a casket.' How do you like the train?"

"It's OK," said Raveendran. "I've heard it said that it's the only civilized way to travel."

"I wouldn't know about that," the man said. "I'm the only one in my family who didn't finish college. I was going to be a lawyer," he looked sideways. "I wunner if the snack bar is open yet. People are taking the stairs. I'm Lee, by the way. I don't care about your name," he said with a wink. "I'll never see you again after I get off in Los Angeles."

Los Angeles! Raveendran already dreaded spending the trip to Albuquerque, much less the whole trip alongside this windbag.

Lee went on, "I had a friend at Wilmington who was a longshoreman. They'd work hard for two hours and then they'd take a two hour beer or whisky break. They'd go back to the parking lot and drink it out of the bottle in their cars. They were union. And they really only worked four hours a day, and the four hours a guy could whittle down to two if he knew what he was doing. That was the thing for me. I figgered who needs a lawyer. A lawyer is dime a dozen and they're all crooked." After a couple more sidelong glances, "You know I'm going to go downstairs and see if the snack bar is open yet."

The morning mists hung over the cornfields. They grew corn not for people but cattle—Raveendran overheard a porter telling another passenger. Wall after green wall of the sentinel stalks passed by as the train rolled on. The unsoft kernels were said to be tough enough to break one's teeth, and they were not sweet. Seeing the stalks made Raveendran start plotting a break from the train. The Amtrak police would find him sitting in the cornfield devouring it from the cob and spitting out teeth.

The man came up the stairs from the snack bar, behind people loaded with cardboard take-out boxes. He came over and handed a Bud tallboy to Raveendran. "Take some peanuts too."

Thoughts of the corn fled. He pounced on the peanuts and ate them gladly.

"Drink up," said the man. "You only live once."

". . .Unless there's reincarnation," Raveendran said.

"So I did the longshoreman thing while my kids were growing up," Lee resumed the moment his bulk hit the seat cushion. "It gave us a good life. Then one day a whole shipping container fell down on top of me, all two tons. I held out as long as I could. See these teeth: I cracked three them keeping that thing up. But it got the better of me, and my fifth vertebrae was crushed. I had to be in a wheelchair for six weeks and then I had a stroke. One thing and another. A friend said Lee, if you didn't have bad luck you wouldn't have any luck at all. I was on the mend and then whammo, heart attack. I had five stents put in my heart."

"You must have a very big heart to have all those tents," Raveendran said after the third sip of beer.

"On top of that I got type three diabetes," Lee said.

Raveendran burped eloquently.

"Well I found out about this thing from my doctor. I don't usually trust these guys; they're usually quacks and crooked. But I did right by him. 'Lee,' he said, 'with all your health problems, we could have you on disability.' So here I am living the life. I take a bus to the Indian casino when I want, and I get to travel Amtrak and see my grandkids in Bakersfield. I wish I'd found out about this job years ago.

"Go ahead," the man said to Ravendreen. "Take half of the candy bar. Go ahead. You only live once. Unless there's reincarnation."

After awhile, Lee stood up from the seat and yawned. Good god, the man was big as a polar bear. He put the faded baseball cap back on the head of dark wavy hair streaked by gray.

"Would you like anything from the snack bar?"

"No thanks," Raveendran said. Lee was so generous, he knew now that Lee would get him anything he asked for. To the vegetarian Raveendran it occurred to ask for a hamburger with the meat patty removed, but that might be too complicated. Then again he wouldn't mind another chocolate bar. Sharing it with his neighbor made it yummy, even if he was breaking his vow to refrain from sugary confections.

Our traveler from the sub-continent took advantage of Lee's departure and left the observation car to make a phone call. Feeling toasty from the tallboy, he walked through the train cars, swayed to and fro like a lotus blossom on an ocean. At the very last car of the train he phoned his rich Uncle Nayan who had made a fortune importing toilet paper from Mexico to a chain-store in the United States. But that was before free-trade and now his uncle was in the motel business, managing a seedy motel in south Los Angeles that catered to couples needing a passion pod.

"We are two hours behind after we waited for a train in Kansas City," Raveendran sighed. "And we lost another 20 minutes in Grand Junction Colorado. We're terribly behind."

"It doesn't matter," said Uncle Nayan calmly. Nayan had seen it all—and a little bit more. "The motel can wait. *You have to pay for the ice: that is the policy.* No, I'm not talking to you, nephew. *I'm talking to YOU, hooligan Get out.*"

"Uncle. . ."

"I'm not talking to you. It's the horrible people who aren't guests and they come to steal our ice."

Raveendran hung up the phone and burped. The funny hat lady who had refused to sell him a few almonds the previous sleepless night was dozing off. The pinkish red cherries would be very nice. They were peeking out of a plastic bag on the seat next to her. He took one with a pang—after all it was a theft, he knew—and it delighted his tongue all the same.

Over the loudspeaker came the announcement that the next stop was Ratón, New Mexico. Here the landscape had changed: the clouds were swirling, soaring and the houses were adobe with logs sticking out of the top. The coarse walls spoke of lives poor but clean. It reminded him of settlements outside of Punjab.

"There will be a brief stop here, to stretch," said the fuzzy loudspeaker voice. "But don't light up. Don't even think about it."

Raveendran stood at the very back of the train and watched, mesmerized, as the ribbon of rails passed behind, all the way to the other end of the continent.

As the Southwest Chief came to a slow stop, the main Western street of Ratón beckoned. In the chalky afternoon sun, there baked a collection of stone and brick buildings on a mesa below outcroppings of hills.

Raveendran took the stairs down to the open hatch on the lower car level, and walked outside. He saw the people, smoke-deprived smokers for the most part, stretching and fingers writhing as they itched to light up. The arid New Mexico air was refreshingly warm compared to the chilly air in the train where the windows couldn't be opened.

Quick as a billy goat, Raveendran loped over rocks on the ground and avoided the small train depot the size of a cabin, locked tight and dead as a museum. Over rocks and crevices he scrambled and saw windows for a market down the dusty street but he didn't trust it; the windows looked blank and papered over and it was too far away to risk it. The train could leave without him. Closer, he saw a bearded man in front of a store, watching the day pass by. His establishment purported to be a general store, if the sign was to be believed. Raveendran's eye was riveted by a hand-lettered sign that said 'apples.'

"An apple!" he said, winded. The man looked at him, squinted, and pointed to an empty box. "Oranges," again the man pointed to emptiness. "Cucumbers."

"Nein."

"Peaches?"

"Nyet," he said. "Mister, I don't know what language you understand. But the produce truck didn't come this week."

The red-bearded man took in the anguish in Raveendran's gaze.

"Look, I can make you a burger," the man said.

That's when Raveendran looked over his shoulder and saw the porter lifting up the stepping stool and the hatch closing with finality. The Southwest Chief had left without Raveendran.

Raveendran's eyes locked onto the dull silver string of cars that constituted the Southwest Chief, chased by a lone sagebrush tumbling down Ratón's main street. The window of the general store supplied a beautiful view. Over the ridge disappeared the last car, and there only remained the rails, silver shiny on top.

"A hamburger," Raveendran said to the red-bearded man and added as an afterthought, "Without the meat."

"Well, then it isn't a hamburger," said the man. "It's a ketchup sandwich."

"I'll have one, please," said Raveendran. A moment earlier he would have skipped the please, frantic over the train's impending departure.

"OK, suit yourself," the man said.

He took his time putting on an apron and tying the knot. He heated up the grill to fry the buns. Raveendran was in no hurry now that the train was gone.

"I missed my train," Raveendran said, while the man check to see if the buns were brown on one side. "When is the next one?"

"Not till tomorrow," said the man. "Think about hitching by the highway."

He paid the gentleman, and out into the street he took his nourishment wrapped in white paper. He thought frankly about throwing the "ketchup sandwich" out, but he had paid the same price as for a hamburger with meat. He was surely becoming American in his twelve days in the country; he was buying things he no desire for, let alone the will to enjoy. Yet once he had acquired it, he was seized by a fiendish possessiveness. He strolled west down the main street, following the direction of the train and the sagebrush.

He walked over the cracked sidewalk, where clumps of weed had their way. In front of the store that said 'Market' there was a sign that extended overhead: FRESH PRO-DUCE. In the papered window was a painting of a turnip with eyes and little feet; in a lower corner was a For Sale sign; it told the full story. Through a tear in the paper Raveendran spied dusty scales hanging in limbo. Between the front windows was a recessed doorway. In the shade a woman crouched.

"It's you," he exclaimed.

"And you!"

It was the bright-eyed woman from the train who'd craved a stalk of celery.

"The train left us in the dirt."

"Here," he extended the bun with the pickle and a dab of ketchup."

"Oh no, I can't have that. It must have glutens."

"If one hungers enough, I suppose one might eat dirt," said Raveendran. "Now what is this terrible menace of glutens which is bringing Western civilization to its knees?"

"Didn't you see the snack bar on the train," she said. "Everything they have has glutens, even the water."

His finger extracted the pickle from the bun smothered in ketchup. "Would you like it?"

"It's loaded with glutens. No thanks," she sneered.

Raveendran took the scalloped pickle and bit into it with great fruition.

"I'm Gloria, by the way," she introduced herself.

"Raveendran, but you can call me Ravi."

"What are we going to do?" she, suddenly hysterical. "I left my phone on the train."

"The next train comes tomorrow at the same time, said the man at the store. If you're in a hurry, we can hitch a ride by the highway, and the way the train is you might even catch up by Albuquerque."

They stood out in the hot sun, sticking their thumbs out. Vacationing families whizzed by and blew off her hat, RVs the size of African republics, motorcyclists on Harleys. Then a red pickup, a dusty unwashed red, passed them by. Then it veered to a halt and backed up. Raveendran jogged up; Gloria followed. The man at the wheel signaled: "One of you sit in back by the toolbox."

"Great scot," said Raveendran. He saw the red T-shirt that said *Keep Calm and Carry On*. "You're the man from the train."

"You're the man who got kicked off for smoking," Gloria exclaimed. "I heard of you. You're famous."

"I jumped off. That was the train from hell," he said, craggy lines showing in his face.

"Now we're stuck in Ratón, New Mexico," said Gloria.

"I'm still pissed off at the way they treated me," he said, sucking on a Marlboro red.

"I'm pissed off about the glutens," said Gloria.

"I'm pissed, as you Americans say, that I can't find an apple," said Raveendran.

"The next long stop is Albuquerque. Hop aboard," said the craggy man. "I'll get you there. I'm still sore about what happened; I just wanted a smoke."

"I just wanted an apple. A crisp shiny apple," said Raveendran. "By now, I'd do with a mushy apple."

The red pick-up flew along parallel to the train tracks in hopes of catching up with the train that had left Raveendran and Gloria in the dust.

"I've got a plan," said the man in the red T-shirt intent behind the wheel. Name of Rusty, corroborated by the flaking cursive letters painted on the side of his truck: *Rusty Nails' Roofing*.

"What's the plan?" Gloria the Gluten-Phobe was able to say in a quieter stretch between Ratón and Las Vegas, New Mexico. Rusty, former country lounge singer and current psycho roofer, pointed to the message on his shirt: *Keep Calm and Carry On*.

"I'll stick to the second part of the equation," said Rusty. "Calm will git you nowhere. That's my plan when we catch up with the Southwest Chief in Las Vegas."

On they sped to Las Vegas, New Mexico. In the course of their approach, they hit a particularly acute bump.

"How are you back there, Ravine?" Gloria shouted from the cab with its dust-caked windows.

Raveendran moaned from his place in the back beside Rusty's toolbox and flame-thrower.

They turned a corner and there was the sleepy station. The pick-up screeched to a halt, Rusty Nails jumped out and peered up and down the length of the tracks.

"Where's the train to Los Angeles?" Rusty asked a man sitting on a suitcase.

"Already left," said a bear of a man. "I got thrown off the train."

Raveendran looked and saw it was Lee, his talkative partner from the observation car.

"I got thrown off the train." That was vintage Lee, repeating the same thing in the hope that it would be mistaken for a new thought.

"No kidding," Raveendran interjected slang remembered from American movies. That terse 'no kidding' concealed sudden warmth for Lee, whom Raveendran now welcomed as a long lost brother.

"I decided to smoke some grass, strictly medicinal," said Lee. "I have a prescription and everything—for my lower back pain from when the shipping container fell on me. Hey, I got something for you," Lee winked. From his pocket he pulled a candy bar and a tallboy.

"There isn't time for that," said Rusty. "Let's hop aboard my rig."

Before starting back on the road, Rusty went alongside the baking station—he could feel the heat radiated from the hot stucco—and stole the lids from old metal garbage cans.

"These will be our shields. You hop aboard the payload with Randy there," he said to Lee.

When Lee slid/rolled into the back of the pickup, the suspension took a big dip.

"We've got a righteous cause, gentlemen and lady," said Rusty. "We've been harassed and persecuted because we're rebels, because we're round pegs in a square world, because we smoke and stink up wherever we go and the second-hand smoke shortens lives."

"We have suffered," Gloria spoke, "the torture of glutens."

"We have suffered," Raveendran spoke, "because we cannot find the vegetables we seek. I have not been able to hold to my vow to eat nature's bounty."

"You both oughta sue Amtrak," Lee said. "It'll be good for you, Ravine. Get a lawsuit going and you'll be more than halfway to becoming American."

The sun blazed, the wind blew and as the afternoon matured, shadows of the hills flashed against their pickup. Soon after a sign announced the onset of Albuquerque, Rusty chauffeured them to a smoke shop that sold cartons of cigarettes and at a farmers market near the train station, they stocked up on big sacks stuffed with carrots, celery and tomatoes. The back of the pickup was so full now, Raveendran and Lee had to travel standing up, propped on the metal frame that squared off the payload. Rusty, looking as stony and determined as one of the faces on Mount Rushmore, drove doggedly on.

"Ee haa!" shouted Gloria, as Rusty's red pickup sped over stretches of what had once been Route 66. "We're bringing relief and salvation to the prisoners aboard the Southwest Chief. Vegetables and fresh smokes."

Rusty added, "I've got a flame thrower to install torch-down roofing. If we encounter resistance, it'll come in handy."

So it was, beefy Lee, Gloria the Gluten-Phobe, Rusty the Roofer and Raveendran Patel, this band of smokers and vegetarians who had been kicked off or left behind by the Southwest Chief, this small yet fierce alliance pulled up to the Albuquerque station and hopped out (slid out in the case of Lee). They lugged bags bulging with American Spirit cigarettes and organic carrots, squash and diverse fruit. Led by Rusty, they ran stealthily down the side of the station.

"Train here yet?" they asked the vendors of Navajo rugs

and turquoise.

"It's coming," they said.

This instilled confidence in the band of rebels who only wanted to be free to puff their own toxins or be free of the packaged toxins sold in the snack shop. They waited on the platform and kept glancing at the perspective where the rails vanished in the east. This could mean, arrest, jail time, and even being banned from ever traveling on Amtrak again, but they were a group of Americans committed to their pleasures and freedoms. Even Raveendran, the Indian first-time traveler in America.

From faraway over the New Mexico landscape lobbed the toots of a train whistle. This mournful sound was mixed with a riotous dinging of trestle bells.

Gloria, Raveendran, Lee and Rusty held their garbage can shields aloft, ready for action. The passenger train was preceded by a smoke plume that shot up straight into the platinum blue sky. That was odd since the Chief wasn't pulled by a steam locomotive. The closer the train got, the more obvious the source of the smoke became. Flames from the observation car were licking the sky. The bells clang-clanged, the train lumbered forward and screeched to a stop. It made a deep groaning sound and wheezed as a tire losing all its air.

Passengers came out choking, some limping, others running. An elderly man with a kerchief over his mouth was helped off by porters on either side. The sirens got louder as firetrucks and ambulances moved in. Stretchers were hoisted onto the platform.

Raveendran held onto Gloria's hand. It seemed the right thing to do. The heat from the burning observation car made sweat bead on her forehead, and both felt the flames' warmth, beyond that of the setting sun, on their faces and shoulders.

"Great scot," said Raveendran, "what happened?"

"There was a coalition between the smokers and the vegetarians." It was the woman with the funny hat who had denied Raveendran the almonds the first night out of Chicago. "It was horrifying. Even a few rogue Boy Scouts joined in. They disabled the porters using foam from fire extinguishers. They seized the observation car. Then the vegheads looted all the tomatoes and lettuce from the dining car coolers. Somehow the upholstery in the observation car caught on fire as the smokers puffed away."

Rusty thrust his garbage can shield down onto the platform overrun by dazed passengers and rescue workers.

"Darn! Someone stole my idea."

From one of the big sacks of fruit and cigarettes there rolled a single green apple. Raveendran picked it up gently and took a refreshing bite out of it.

"Here," he handed it to Gloria. "It's gluten free, and so am I."

They finished the apple together. When the apple was all gone, Raveendran planted the first of many kisses on Gloria and drew her close to him.

THE END?

Photo by Don Goodman

about the author

Graydon Miller grew up in Watsonville, California. He attended local schools and later went to New York's Columbia University, which he fled before graduating. His stories and humor pieces appear in numerous publications, including *The Cynic*, *The Morning News*, and *Ellery Queen*. He is the author of the acclaimed story collection *The Havana Brotherhood* (available on Amazon). He lives in Hollywood.